EVERY NIGHT
AT THE
LONDON PALLADIUM

EVERY NIGHT
AT THE
LONDON PALLADIUM

Patrick Pilton

 Robson Books

FIRST PUBLISHED IN GREAT BRITAIN IN 1976 BY
ROBSON BOOKS LTD., 28 POLAND STREET, LONDON
W1V 3DB. COPYRIGHT © 1976 PATRICK PILTON.

ISBN 0 903895 77 3

Printed in Great Britain by Redwood Burn Ltd., Trowbridge.

Contents

Preface

The London Palladium is the greatest Variety theatre in the world. In the days when every major provincial city boasted its Empire or its Palace or its Hippodrome, the Palladium was the number one booking — the Mecca every young performer aspired to, the flagship of the fleet on which second-raters were never invited to sail. Ask any artist who has appeared at the Palladium and he or she will tell you that the real star is the theatre itself.

'I could never go on at the Palladium and just *walk* through a show,' says Harry Secombe. 'I'd feel that the ghosts of the past which inhabit the place would gang up and turn on me.'

Gracie Fields admits: 'I was always a mass of nerves. I couldn't think of anything or anybody else. I always demanded so much of myself at the Palladium — it was Number One, and you had to give the audience something different.'

'It never loses its magic,' says Dorothy Squires. 'This is Mecca — there isn't a place like it in the whole world.'

In July 1974 Debbie Reynolds was asked to sacrifice her first holiday in two years to make her Palladium début. She was exhausted after an arduous season in Reno, and asked for time to think the offer over. Finally, she agreed. 'Though had it been any other theatre but the Palladium,' she said, 'my answer would have been "No".'

The proudest possession in the homes of many international

stars is the Palladium Oscar — the brass nameplate screwed to the dressing-room door and presented to every top of the bill at the end of a show's run.

Impressionist Peter Goodwright rushed his new-born baby to the theatre, pushed the pram onto the revolving stage, and had the stagehands spin it round. 'Now he'll always be able to say he has appeared at the Palladium,' he explained delightedly.

One middle-aged hopeful auditioning at the Palladium for the television talent show 'New Faces', walked on stage and did absolutely nothing. After a long pause, he glanced down at producer Les Cocks in the stalls and said: 'Thank you. I know my act isn't good enough for your show, so I won't bother you. I just wanted to tell my grandchildren that I had been on the stage at the London Palladium.'

Such is the awe in which this great theatre is held. . .

This book is not a history, but rather a collection of stories — some humorous, some touching, some recording great moments of triumph, others recalling failure and disaster. The stories were related to me by the stars who have appeared at the Palladium and by the loyal staff who work there. To them, my thanks.

Theatre Notes

On 4 March 1935 a revue opened at the London Palladium called 'Life Begins at Oxford Circus'. It had been assembled in ten days by three enthusiastic young bloods while the Guv'-nor, George Black, was sunning himself on a six weeks' cruise to the West Indies. So elaborate were the sets that the dress rehearsal lasted from 10 am on Monday until 6 am the following morning. In one scene, 'The Musicians' Dream', members of the orchestra flew above the stage suspended on wires.

On his return a startled George Black berated his young assistants — Val Parnell, Charles Henry and band leader and impresario Jack Hylton — but secretly he had to admit that 'Life Begins at Oxford Circus' was quite something, and in the event all he altered was a lighting spot or two.

The revue starred the Crazy Gang, and a feature of the show was a spectacular opening sequence in which the theatre's elevator stage was used for the first time. Everyone taking part in the scene — including the band — made their entrance in the guise of commuters emerging from the depths of Oxford Circus underground station.

Today, two-thirds of the 2,317 patrons who can pack the theatre at each performance arrive through the gateway of Oxford Circus tube. The station exit you want is Argyll Street. Turn left, past a restaurant designed as a Kentucky paddle-steamer, past a tiny shop where they sell mouth-water-

13

ing home-made chocolates in fancy boxes, past a snack bar where the hungry stare like goldfish through a plate-glass window as they munch away at their hamburgers.

Round the corner in once-trendy Carnaby Street, at The Shakespeare's Head or The Dog and Trumpet, you might catch one of the cast sinking a quick pint before the curtain goes up. In the interval, or while a comedian is holding the stage, you will certainly catch the band there. 'Safe for a quick one, here' is a frequent annotation in an artist's band parts.

The Palladium building is an imposing grey structure, smaller perhaps than you might have imagined, all porches and pillars and Edwardian elegance. Daydream, and you are transported to an era of gas lamps and hansom cabs, with royalty and fine ladies descending the red-carpeted steps under the protective glass canopy that stretches out into the roadway. Blink, and you are back in the bustle of Regent Street, with the burlesque of the buskers and the bright lights of the hoardings, where the star of the show smiles down invitingly, enticing you inside.

Stalls to your left, via the Variety Bar with its illuminated black and white sketches of past Palladium stars — George Formby, Max Miller, Gracie Fields, Laurel and Hardy — and old black and red theatre bills bearing magical and sometimes mysterious names — whatever happened to Lowe, Burnoff and Wensley?

Circle to your right, up the stairs into the stylish, more relaxed atmosphere of the Cinderella Bar where on the Monday before the opening of a new show the stars meet the Press, and where, the rest of the week, Rose and Leila serve gin and tonic and Bacardi and Coke to the patrons and wish that every week was a Tom Jones week: 'The place is packed, then. Our takings shoot up — and we go home with a nice bonus at the end of it.'

Palladium manager John Avery, in formal dinner dress, is watching over the hustle and bustle in the foyer as the 6.15 audience comes out and the 8.45 one goes in. 'We've been known to empty the theatre and fill it again in ten minutes,' he says. 'But that is really shifting them.'

14

In George Black's day the star of the show would be encouraged to join the manager in greeting the theatregoers. A night at the London Palladium was an occasion, Black preached, an evening of anticipation and wonderment. On stage, and in the auditorium, only the best was good enough for the Palladium.

There was one occasion, however, when Black's showmanship did not turn out as planned. A special welcome was prepared for the millionth customer to see the Palladium show 'The Little Dog Laughed'. The stars of the show, the Crazy Gang, waited beside the box office until they received the signal that the magic million had been reached.

The winners were a middle-aged couple. The Gang shook them warmly by the hand and presented the lady with a huge bouquet and the man with a box of cigars. Instead of being shown to the seats they had paid for, the couple were escorted to Black's personal theatre box. During the interval they were taken backstage for a drink with the artists. The Guv'nor had invited half of Fleet Street to the ceremony.

When the couple saw the photographers they looked aghast. 'Oh, my!' exclaimed the man. 'I can't have my picture taken. 'I've only just met the lady — ten minutes ago, at Oxford Circus. Whatever will my wife say?'

Yes, life — and the London Palladium — begins at Oxford Circus!

The Palladium stands where once stood the town residence of the Duke of Argyll. Next door lived the Duke of Marlborough. In the early 1800s, the Duke of Argyll's residence was sold to another Scottish laird, the fourth Earl of Aberdeen, who was Prime Minister of Britain from 1852 to 1855. When he died in 1860, the house was sold to a firm of wine and spirit merchants. The wines were stored in vaults twenty-five feet below ground, while above them, but still below ground, a second level housed a bazaar.

The bazaar was not a success, and in 1871 Frederick Charles Hengler signed a ten-year lease on the site to establish a London base for his popular and profitable touring circus. There were performances every evening at 7.30, with matinées each Wednesday and Saturday. Seats cost from one shilling to five shillings — half price if you arrived after nine o'clock. After Hengler's death, apart from a period when the site was converted into the National Ice Skating Palace, a succession of circuses invaded Argyll Street — from Italy, from France, and even from Russia.

By 1908 the building was in dire need of repair. London Theatres of Variety decided to purchase the premises, demolish them and build the largest and grandest music hall the capital had yet seen, a hall more luxurious than Edward Moss's Hippodrome, Oswald Stoll's Coliseum and Alfred Butt's Palace put together. A leading theatre architect, Frank Matcham, was assigned £250,000 to build an auditorium of the utmost luxury and comfort. The Palladium, as it was called, was the first London theatre to be carpeted throughout, the first to install tip-up seats, and the absence of pillars gave the entire audience an unrestricted view of the stage.

On Boxing Night, 1910, the conductor raised his baton to lead the orchestra into the specially-composed 'Palladium March', and the curtain went up on the first Palladium show.

Since that opening night, the fortunes of the theatre have revolved largely around six men — the 'Guv'nors' as they became known in the business: Walter Gibbons, the visionary who conceived and built the theatre; Charles Gulliver, who, true to his name, travelled the world in search of fresh talent; George Black, the master showman with the common touch who made Variety synonymous with the Palladium; Val Parnell, who achieved for the theatre its international reputation; Leslie Macdonnell, who met the TV challenge of the 'sixties; and Louis Benjamin, who enticed the superstars back to the Palladium.

Walter Gibbons had seemed destined for a career in engineering, until he fell in love with Nellie Payne, daughter of George Adney Payne, one of the leading Variety managers of his day. Walter and Nellie married in 1902, and Payne immediately set about — and succeeded in — interesting his son-in-law in a

The greatest Variety theatre in the world

Three stars of the 1948 Royal Variety Show:

Betty Hutton discusses her act with Val Parnell . . .

Julie Andrews (her Palladium début) . . .

and G. H. Elliott, 'the Chocolate Coloured C

Danny Kaye slumps exhaustedly after his triumphant Palladium début...

...and Frankie Howerd catnaps during rehearsals for the 1950 Royal Variety Show

(Daily Mail)

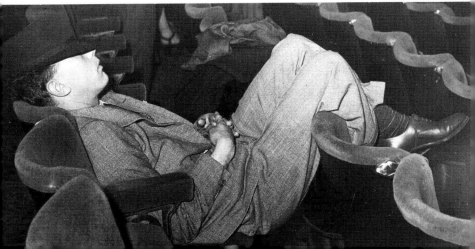

*The Royal Box in
1930 . . .*

and in 1972

(Joe Matthews)

scheme to rescue several suburban music halls that had fallen on bad times. Gibbons formed a public company — the London Theatres of Variety Limited — to take over the halls and run them as one large circuit. Fourteen theatres in and around the capital were purchased, and their close proximity to each other meant that the same artist could play two or three venues on the same night.

Investors showed little interest in the scheme, but a sufficient number of patrons handed over their sixpences at the box office to make LTV a going concern. However, the suburban circuit was not grandiose enough for Gibbons. He set his heart on building a new theatre in the centre of London. In November 1908, Gibbons, auctioneer Sidney Marler, lawyer Arthur Copson Peake and song-writer George Dance, formed Capital Syndicate Limited, and took an option on the Hengler Circus site.

Like a doting father with his new offspring, Gibbons spent lavishly and extravagantly on his London Palladium. Warnings of impending disaster went unheeded. He would engage more acts than he needed to fill a bill and, after the opening night, pack off those who had received the least applause to his suburban halls. It cost him £600 to persuade Edyth Walker, the American prima donna, to transfer from Covent Garden to the Palladium for one week's Variety. Soon it became obvious that Gibbons was not the man to establish the Palladium on a firm financial footing.

Approaches were made to LTV's great rival, Sir Oswald Stoll, whose own circuit revolved around the Coliseum and was enjoying considerable success. Sir Oswald agreed to take time off to run the LTV company, but with one proviso — Gibbons would have to go. It took six months for the power game to be played out, but early in 1912 a dejected Walter Gibbons, his dream shattered, sold his shares and announced that he was resigning 'owing to ill health'. Stoll was by now firmly established on the board, along with a bright young man of twenty-nine called Charles Gulliver who had been employed as the company secretary.

It was Gulliver who now took charge of the London Theatres of Variety operation and made the Palladium a viable proposition once again. Ballet, operetta, playlets, musical comedy, melodrama, slapstick and revue became strange bedfellows as the new Guv'nor fought to win back the customers. When the Tango became the rage, patrons took 'Tango Teas' in the foyer and danced on stage with the performers. When fighting broke out in the Balkans, Gulliver engaged a war correspondent to give daily news commentaries illustrated with slides. Captain Scott's expedition to the South Pole was faithfully relayed on a bioscope.

Most theatres had by now discarded the traditional vaudeville format, and shows began to be entities with titles and storylines. Occasionally a revue intruded into a Palladium season, but in the main Gulliver stayed faithful to the musichall artists who had served him well in the past, such as Harry 'Stiffy the Goalkeeper' Weldon; Lorna and Toots Pound (mimics and dancers from Australia); eccentric comedian Will Evans; G.H. Elliott, the Chocolate Coloured Coon; husband and wife singing act J.W. Tate and Clarice Mayne; Albert Whelan, the first artist to make an entrance to a signature tune; and Little Tich, the crazy comic who danced in boots that were more akin to water skis. When Gulliver was able to book her, Marie Lloyd packed 'em in with 'The Boy I Love is up in the Gallery', and George Robey, of the heavy eyebrows and cleric's coat, had them chortling with his clever characterisations and comic songs.

Gulliver's perseverance paid off. London Theatres of Variety prospered, bought out one of its rivals, and the Palladium became firmly established as a leading music hall. Gulliver was becoming a much-respected impresario, quick to sense changes in the public mood. He realised that the formula that had taken the Palladium successfully through the war years was not in tune with the Roaring Twenties. The new decade called for entertainment that was more outrageous, that had dash and verve, colour and costume, music and dancing. In one word — something *spectacular!*

Gulliver teamed up with Harry Day, doyen of the touring revue, and together they staged a series of spectacular revues.

There was 'Rockets', which ran for five hundred performances and, according to one critic, 'almost took one's breath away'. Then there was 'Whirl of the World' with Nellie Wallace, Billy Merson and Tommy Handley (and sketches by Edgar Wallace), which played 627 performances, creating a record that survived for twenty years. 'Sky High' followed, then an English version of the 'Folies Bergère'.

The year 1927 saw the first Palladium musical, 'Apache', featuring a handsome ex-boxer from Denmark called Carl Brisson. But the tide was beginning to turn. While 'Apache' was playing the Palladium, talking pictures were invading Broadway.

The stage was set for Walter Gibbons to return.

After his departure in 1912 Gibbons had returned to his first love — films. Before his marriage he had toured the halls showing moving pictures from a bioscope. A small boy would operate the projector while Gibbons stood beside the screen, speaking the commentary. For many years he tried unsuccessfully to synchronise the films to gramophone records. Once he even persuaded Vesta Tilley to sing a song over and over again while he both photographed and recorded it. But for all his experiments, Gibbons never did discover a method of linking the picture to the sound.

It was ironic, then, that sixteen years after his ignominious departure, Gibbons — now Sir Walter Gibbons — should return to the Palladium and convert it into a cinema. He found the financial backing to re-acquire his beloved theatre, as well as the other LTV interests. It had cost him £250,000 to build the Palladium; he bought it back for £1,570,000.

There was one stumbling block to his plan. The company which enjoyed the concession to sell programmes and chocolates at the Palladium took Sir Walter to court, claiming that the change in function would ruin their business. 'Is it impossible to consume chocolates in the darkness?' asked the judge. 'No!' replied Sir Walter, and won his case.

He formed the General Theatres Corporation, and on 19 March 1928, the Palladium staged its first cine-Variety show: three hours of films and music hall.

A controversial British film called *Dawn*, about the death of Nurse Edith Cavell, was to lead to Sir Walter's second downfall. Foreign Secretary Sir Austen Chamberlain persuaded the censors to ban the film following protests from the German Embassy that it was anti-German. The London County Council were not convinced and decided to determine the issue for themselves. After an all-night sitting the Council granted the film a licence to be shown in London – and Sir Walter paid a record sum to secure it for the Palladium.

Not for the first time Gibbons had spent foolishly. Ten days later the film was transferred to another theatre, and the discord that had been simmering in the GTC boardroom for some time boiled over. Once again Sir Walter's fellow directors were calling for his resignation; once again he announced his departure 'owing to ill health'.

Sir Walter was bitter. 'I got out because I will not be overridden by amateurs,' he said. He died in 1933, leaving just £90 in cash – and the finest Variety theatre in the world.

George Black, like Gulliver before him, was waiting in the wings at Gibbons' second inglorious exit.

The Palladium his once again, Gibbons had expanded his empire by buying out a northern circuit of cine-Variety theatres run by three brothers – George, Alfred and Ted Black. The three agreed to sell on condition that George was offered a job with Gibbons in London. 'The Palladium was going through a terribly bad patch', recalls George Black's younger son Alfred, now a leading impresario himself. 'They told Dad, "The Palladium is yours – do something with it".'

Black determined to make it the number one Variety theatre of the world. His first task was to persuade the people of London, who had become apathetic to the music hall, that Variety was far from dead. For weeks the capital was plastered with black and yellow posters mysteriously proclaiming 'Variety is coming back'. Later the words 'To the Palladium' were added.

The old axiom 'it pays to advertise' worked. His new Variety season opened on 3 September 1928. Curtain up for the first house was scheduled for 6.10 pm; by ten in the morning there were long queues outside the theatre for tickets. They came for Variety, and Variety they got. On the programme were: The Seven Hindustans (acrobats); Dick Henderson ('Yorkshire comedian'); Adam, Amelia and Marti di Gatano (dancers); Ann Codee ('French comedienne'); Ivor Novello and Phyllis Monkman in Novello's one-act play *The Gate Crasher;* Tamara ('trapeze artiste'); the Runaway Four ('comedy dancers'); Gracie Fields (her Palladium début); Billy Bennett ('almost a gentleman'); and Alfred Jackson's Sixteen English Dancing Girls.

A first-class bill was not sufficient for Black. He insisted on elaborate sets, swirling drapes, colourful costumes. A set was even especially created for the top of the bill.

Gracie Fields was overawed by it all. Presented with a fabulous new creation to wear, she came on from the back of the stage through rows of pale mauve swathes, swags and chiffon, threw her jade green scarf on the piano, sighed, and told the audience: 'Eee, by gum. It's all too grand for me.'

The giant Gaumont-British Picture Corporation − which had seized control of Gibbons's General Theatres Corporation in 1929 − bought a controlling interest in the rival Moss Empires theatre group. The twelve GTC theatres were merged with the thirty or so Moss halls, and Black, the man who had revitalised the Palladium, was given control of the lot.

The vast Moss circuit gave Black a new outlet for his talents. The names of the glittering productions he had presented still stir the hearts of the millions who saw them: 'Black Velvet', 'Black Vanities', 'London Rhapsody', 'These Foolish Things' − names which revive nostalgic memories of a theatrical age long past.

Black was a strict disciplinarian. Artists were always on their best behaviour when GB (as he was affectionately known) was in the theatre. And an artist always knew just when that was, for Black's one touch of ostentation gave him away. Although he always sat well back in his favourite Palladium box, the glow of his fat cigar was clearly visible to anyone performing on stage. When that cigar glowed, the curtain always went up to the second, no act ever over-ran, and any dubious lines a comic might be tempted to include were kept for another night.

Black died on 4 March 1945. In his Palladium dressing-room Tommy Trinder smashed a glass — the Guv'nor's glass. Black would be a tough act to follow.

Val Parnell was, if anything, even more tenacious and un-yielding than his illustrious predecessor. As the boss of the great Moss Empires chain at a time when the live theatre was an entertainer's main source of income, Parnell wielded great power and was thus in a position to make a number of enem-ies. An irate performer once arrived at the Palladium brandish-ing a revolver and threatening to shoot him. Parnell sent the man a note: 'For that privilege,' it read, 'you will have to wait your turn in a pretty lengthy queue.'

Stars, it was said, merely bowed to royalty — to Val Parnell they knelt. And it was easier to gain an audience with the monarch than to see Parnell's booking manager, Cissie Wil-liams.

Parnell, of the boxer's profile and wrestler's physique, was a gargantuan man in every sense of the word. He was both feared and revered in the profession. Members of staff signall-ed the news of his arrival at the Palladium to each other by whistling a few bars of 'Stormy Weather'.

'He was strict, but fair,' says the present Palladium manag-ing director, Louis Benjamin. 'This is a tough profession. Artists must have an ego or they wouldn't be in the business. Parnell laid down the ground rules. If an artist broke them he was likely to find himself without a livelihood.'

One who did break the rules was an American comedian named Jackie Miles, and it was his first appearance at the Palladium. Parnell told him to do eleven minutes. When he got on stage Miles carried on for an extra nine minutes. Between houses Parnell confronted the comic. Miles in-sisted that his act was going so well it was impossible for him to leave the stage. Parnell was adamant that he should keep to eleven minutes. Next house, Miles stayed on stage even longer — twenty-four minutes. When he came off Parnell stormed into the dressing-room and bel-lowed, 'You're out!' Miles received his £600 salary, but he never played the London Palladium again.

Parnell possessed a soft side, too. Once he gave a chorus line an entire week off in the middle of a production because they had been working so hard. On another occasion, heading home after an arduous tour and half-asleep in the back of his car, Parnell suddenly remembered that he had promised to watch a young comedian's act. He ordered his chauffeur to turn around and take him back to the theatre.

Val Parnell was born into the business. His father was Fred Russell, editor of the *Hackney Gazette,* who turned ventriloquist in the 1890s and toured the world with his dummy, Coster Joe. Russell felt unable to use his real surname because an Irish politician of the day, Charles Stewart Parnell, was in disrepute over a divorce action being brought against him. Russell feared the scandal associated with the name Parnell would adversely affect his career.

Young Val chose the back-room side of show business, working his way from office boy at thirteen and selling tickets at the Camberwell Empire, to booking acts for Vesta Tilley's husband, Sir Walter de Frece. It was Charles Gulliver who recruited Parnell to the Palladium hierarchy. In 1922 Gibbons retained him as booking manager to implement his cine-Variety policy, and when Black took over he made Parnell his general manager.

In June 1945 the line 'Val Parnell presents. . .' first appeared on a Palladium poster. The show was 'High Time'. Parnell's first innovation was to put the clocks back. The wartime blackout had forced theatre managements to time their performances for around 2.30 pm and 5.15 pm. Parnell decided it was 'high time' to revert to a late evening show, and re-timed his second house for 8.30 pm.

A second innovation was more controversial — the importation of Hollywood film stars to top the Palladium bill. From 1948 to 1952 came a procession of stars like Carmen Miranda, Pearl Bailey, Edgar Bergen and Charlie McCarthy, Jack Benny, The Andrews Sisters, Dinah Shore, Betty Hutton, Ella Fitzgerald, George Burns and Gracie Allen, Benny Goodman, Buddy Greco, Larry 'Al Jolson' Parks, Frank Sinatra,

27

Abbott and Costello, Lena Horne, Nat King Cole, Hoagy Carmichael, Judy Garland, Red Skelton, Billy Daniels, Jimmy 'Schnozzle' Durante, Guy Mitchell, Frankie Laine, and many, many more. Critics complained that home-grown talent was being ignored, that screen idols were not necessarily good music-hall material, and that some of the artists were second-raters anyway. The public, it was argued, was being sold short. Parnell replied that he would dearly love to promote British talent. But how many home-grown stars could fill the Palladium twice nightly, six days a week?

Many aficionados still regard the late 1940s and early 'fifties as the heyday of the Palladium. Certainly the theatre gained its world-wide reputation then, and a seat at the Palladium became a guarantee of the very best in entertainment.

In 1948 Parnell revived the pantomime. He selected the most popular fairy tale of all, 'Cinderella', with Tommy Trinder as Buttons, Zoë Gail as Dandini, and George and Bert Bernard as the Ugly Sisters. 'Puss in Boots' followed, then 'Babes in the Wood' and 'Humpty Dumpty'.

Variety bills were interspersed with colourful revues: 'Sky High' with Charlie Chester; 'Out of This World' with Frankie Howerd; 'The Peep Show' ('an eyeful and earful of great entertainment') with Vera Lynn, which went on to play Broadway; 'Fun and the Fair' with George Formby; and in 1954, a show with a title that would attract a somewhat different audience today: 'The Gay Palladium Show'.

While George Black had his Palladium box, Parnell had a favourite seat — Number 16, Row S, in the stalls. 'I'm Woolworth-minded,' he said. 'I cater for the masses.'

Parnell's flair for mixing a perfect Variety cocktail earned him the title 'Mr Showbusiness'. In 1960 he left Moss Empires to devote all his attention to television. He died in 1972, after a period of failing health. The inscription on a crystal paper-weight that always stood on his desk might well serve as his epitaph. It read: 'To the real star of the Palladium, Val Parnell. From Frank Sinatra.'

In 1960 Moss Empires — who had swapped their cinemas for the General Theatre Corporation's theatres — were brought under the control of Prince Littler's Stoll Theatre Corporation after a battle with millionaire property tycoons Charles Clore and Jack Cotton. Four years later Associated Television bought a controlling interest in the company, and it remains the majority shareholder under its present chairman, Sir Lew Grade.

British entertainers dominated the Palladium during the 'sixties as Leslie Macdonnell persevered with the 'panto-summer revue-Variety' policy of his predecessor, Parnell. The productions became more lavish, more costly and longer-running as the entrepreneurs strove to recoup their investment. In order to woo the public from their cosy firesides, familiar television artists topped the Palladium bills: Frankie Vaughan in 'Startime', Cliff Richard and the Shadows in 'Stars in Your Eyes', Harry Secombe in 'Let Yourself Go', Charlie Drake as the 'Man In The Moon', and Bruce Forsyth, Ken Dodd and Max Bygraves in their own colourful revues.

Under the direction of the present Palladium Guv'nor, Louis Benjamin, 1976 saw the leading international stars return to the Palladium — even if the shows were more Las Vegas in style, with three acts on the bill, than good old-fashioned vaudeville. Benjamin persuaded Shirley MacLaine to make her first stage appearance outside the United States at the Palladium. The critics were ecstatic: 'The stalls, full of celebrities, were a standing mass of cheering fans' . . . 'the long-forgotten Palladium roar was back' . . . 'in twenty-five years of covering the Palladium, I can't think of any woman performer to equal her'. Shirley's success attracted other top-liners to London. She was followed at the Palladium by Eddie Fisher and Lorna Luft, John Denver, Sacha Distel, Tony Bennett and Lena Horne, Joel Gray, The Three Degrees, Julie Andrews, Bing Crosby, Johnnie Ray and Billy Daniels, Charles Aznavour, Sammy Davis Junior, The Carpenters — and even a sprinkling of 'culture' when Sir Robert Helpmann and the Australian Ballet presented a stunningly beautiful production of Franz Lehar's 'The Merry Widow'.

Suddenly the Palladium — and its stars — were front page news again!

Every morning Sir Lew Grade receives a telephone call from Louis Benjamin, who is also managing director of another ATV company, Pye Records. 'Whatever business we have to discuss,' says Benjamin, 'the first question Sir Lew always asks is: "How much did the Palladium take last night?" '

In the great Grade Galaxy, the Palladium is still the brightest star.

Overture

It is close to midnight. Focused in the spotlight on the stage of the London Palladium stands a young man with carroty hair, a clownish face and long, slim-fingered, expressive hands. His head is bowed; tears and perspiration fuse and slowly trickle down his cheeks. The audience — three thousand of them, packed so tightly they spill over into the orchestra pit — are singing 'For He's A Jolly Good Fellow'. The young man sinks to his knees, stretches out his arms and clasps the eager hands that reach out to him.

The tune changes. Now they are singing 'Auld Lang Syne'. So emotionally-charged is the atmosphere, it might be International Day at Cardiff Arms Park or the Last Night of the Proms.

For two magic hours this disarming young man has held his audience spellbound — eighty minutes longer than the time allotted him on the running order pinned up at the side of the stage.

Around 11.30 pm he called out: 'Anybody wanna go home?'

The answer came back, a deafening 'No!'

'What about your last buses and tubes?' — 'We'll *walk* home!'

In the audience are men and women who have queued outside the theatre for two days and two nights to see their idol. The Palladium boss, Val Parnell, pleaded with them to go home, promising to guarantee them tickets, but they stayed just the same. The discomfort of getting home is nothing to the sacrifice they have already made to see this young American.

He has sung a bit; danced a bit; clowned a bit; dangled his legs over the apron of the stage and engaged in extemporary conversation with his audience; he has smoked their proffered cigarettes and even observed the traditional British custom of halting proceedings to drink a cup of tea. He has burlesqued a crooner trying to sing 'Begin the Beguine' but never quite hitting the right note. He has been a coal-black mammy, an operatic tenor with a cold in the nose, a coloratura soprano *almost* hitting top C, a German with a cleft palate, an excitable Italian and a baby in a temper. A lilting Irish ballad, 'In Dublin's Fair City', brought a lump to the audience's throats; a comedy song, 'Minnie the Moocher', brought laughter to their lips. Finally, he has been the personable young man who sends girls into ecstasy — one ardent admirer is seeing the show for the seventeenth time in the six weeks the artist has been at the theatre. She has even climbed the fire escape and broken into his dressing-room to tell him how wonderful he is.

Now, as the applause dies down, the young man turns to his pianist, Sammy Prager (for the first time in the Palladium's history the full orchestra is on stage with the artist). 'My pipes are going', he says. Then, sensing the disappointment in the stalls, adds, 'But I'll stay here as long as I can make an intelligible noise.'

Finally, the orchestra plays the National Anthem. The plush red velvet curtain drops with a finality that says 'enough is enough'. The young entertainer walks slowly to his dressing-room, slumps into a chair and bursts into tears.

'What can I say?' he inquires of a reporter. 'This public has got me. For six weeks I have had nothing but warmth and generosity. Tonight I feel like crying like a baby.'

In the auditorium the reluctant stragglers still shout for more. Outside in Argyll Street extra police have been drafted in to control the waiting throng.

It is the early hours of Sunday morning now. The stage door opens and a lean figure is hustled into a waiting car. A cheer resounds through the night air. Women in the crowd blow kisses. The artist is drained, emotionally and physically, but he waves his hand and smiles.

This is the stuff dreams are made of, fairy tales written about. On this night, 13 March 1948, David Daniel Kominsky — alias Danny Kaye — a Russian Jew from the tough immigrant East-side of New York, won himself a place in the annals of showbusiness legend.

Danny Kaye was the second missile in the armoury with which Val Parnell planned to launch his new policy of presenting the biggest names from Hollywood and Broadway at the Palladium.

Parnell had taken over the management of the theatre from George Black, arguably the greatest British showman ever. Black had built his reputation on glamorous and expensive productions and high-speed Variety. His successor looked across the Atlantic to the movie industry. The stars of the celluloid screen, he decided, would appear in the flesh at his London Palladium.

To open his 1948 variety season, Parnell chose as top of the bill a cocky, snub-nosed, former child star named Mickey Rooney. On his arrival in Britain, Rooney brashly announced, 'I can act, sing, dance, write screen plays. I can direct and produce pictures, play tennis and ride horses. I am show business. I know it all.' It was all true, but those were the days before Muhammad Ali and Brian Clough, when the British disliked braggarts, preferring a more diffident, humble approach. And though Rooney sang, danced, joked, played the trumpet, the drums and the piano, and imitated popular American crooners, for one reason or another he failed to communicate with the Palladium audiences. He tried changing his material, but to no avail. During one performance he finally threw his trumpet into the orchestra pit and told Les

Lambert, a trumpet player with the Skyrockets Orchestra, 'Here, it's all yours, boy.'

On the Wednesday of his last week at the theatre, Rooney failed to arrive for the matinée. He was reported to be ill with post-vaccination fever. But Danny Kaye was in the theatre that afternoon. Since his arrival in London the previous weekend, he had spent every spare moment rehearsing, walking about the empty auditorium to get the 'feel' of it, watching Rooney's performances and checking the reactions of the audience. Kaye was apprehensive about his British stage début. He had built up a screen reputation with films like *Up in Arms, The Kid from Brooklyn* and *The Secret Lives of Walter Mitty,* but to theatre audiences he was still an unknown quantity.

Told that Rooney's matinée had been cancelled, Kaye seized his opportunity. The theatre was standing idle, the orchestra was in the pit, and the stage hands were assembled. He asked Parnell for a full rehearsal and the Palladium boss agreed. Those who were present that afternoon came away convinced that here was a performer who was about to take London by storm.

Rooney withdrew from the remaining nine performances, sacrificing £500 in salary, and flew home to the States. British comedian Sid Field, famous for his role as Slasher Green the Spiv, took over the top billing. Field noticed Kaye's nervousness and at each performance tried to lessen the young man's fears by pointing to the box where Kaye always sat, and introducing him as 'the star of next week's show'. On the final night Field persuaded Kaye to step on stage. He was given a tremendous ovation. 'See what warm people they are,' said Field.

Rooney's disappointing three weeks had its repercussions in the box office. Only moderate advance bookings were reported for Danny Kaye's appearances, and the Palladium staff were given handfuls of free tickets to distribute amongst their friends.

On the opening night Kaye was petrified. While Ted Ray walked onto the stage and announced, 'Ladies and gentlemen, I give you Danny Kaye!', the star of the show stood in the wings, paralysed with fright. Charles Henry, the theatre's chief of production, pleaded with him to go out on the stage. Ted Ray looked anxiously towards the prompt corner. The orchestra played the introductory music for a second time. Henry gave Kaye a push . . . and a new music-hall star stumbled awkwardly into the spotlights.

He was dressed casually in sports jacket, brown slacks and brogues. As he stood before the microphone, looking out on the vast auditorium, he said, 'I'm shaking like a leaf, honestly.' Six short words, yet such was the spell they cast on that opening-night audience, they might have been spoken by Merlin himself. All over the house people began to applaud. Starry-eyed girls called to him from the gallery.

'His success was instantaneous, prodigious and well-won,' wrote the critic from the *News Chronicle*, while the London *Evening News* enthused, 'It really seemed as if the roof must go sailing over Oxford Street at any moment.' These first-night notices had the theatre in a state of siege. The 'House Full' posters went up, and the public used every ploy imaginable to get into the theatre and see the show. A couple of smartly-dressed, respectable-looking old ladies pulled the cleverest con-trick of all. They were comfortably installed in their seats when two other people arrived with apparently identical tickets. The date, time and seat numbers were correct and all four tickets appeared absolutely genuine. The assistant manager could not understand how the double booking could have occurred. Then someone thought to glance at the top of the tickets. Those held by the two innocent-looking elderly ladies were for another theatre altogether — the Prince of Wales.

Aristocrats, heads of government and leading figures from the world of show business flocked to see the wonder that was Danny Kaye. Box office records were broken, tickets were fetching £20 on the black market, and Kaye's contract was extended by two weeks. And music-hall history was made on 26 February 1948 when King George VI and Queen Elizabeth, Princess Elizabeth and the Duke of Edinburgh, and Princess Margaret paid the young entertainer the highest compliment of all: for the first time a reigning monarch attended an ordinary Variety bill as opposed to a special performance staged in his honour.

The visit was arranged at short notice after Princess Elizabeth had seen the show and recommended it to her parents. The Royal Box had already been booked for other dignitaries, and the Palladium management was thrown into confusion. As every seat in the house had been sold, too, it was decided to wait until the night and explain the dilemma to the patrons in the front row of the stalls. The house manager approached a small group and apologetically explained that he had some rather distinguished visitors in that night, and wondered whether they would mind giving up their seats. 'Not bloody likely,' came the reply. 'The only person who will get me out of this seat is the King!'

The King enjoyed his new vantage point. 'Why don't you always put me here instead of in a box?' he asked.

On their previous visit Princess Elizabeth and the Duke had gone backstage to sip champagne and chat to Kaye about his success. After a while the Princess had said that it was getting late and she ought to be leaving for the Palace. Glancing at his watch, Prince Philip protested that it was only eleven o'clock. 'Oh, no!' the Princess corrected him. 'It's just gone twenty past,' and she added a disparaging remark about the reliability of his watch.

'All I know,' Prince Philip replied, 'is that it's the watch your mother gave me.'

Danny Kaye was invited to join the royal couple for supper. He declined with the explanation that he had a previous engagement. Later he confessed that there was no other engagement. 'I was just too nervous to accept,' he said.

There was one touch of pathos during Kaye's visit. On the same bill was a veteran music-hall comedian named Scott Saunders, 'the old hawker'. Every night he would trudge wearily off the stage, bemoaning the fact that the audiences had only come to see the star of the show, and hardly raised a titter at his jokes. Then, one night, after the old comedian had taken his bow, a deafening burst of applause broke out. He could hardly believe his ears, but instinctively walked back on stage to acknowledge the ovation. It was only when he looked out at the audience that the truth hit him. People were on their feet clapping and cheering, but the applause was not for him. It was for a crouched figure walking slowly to its seat, cigar in mouth and hand raised in a familiar V-salute. It was Winston Churchill: out of respect for the performer on stage, he had waited patiently at the back of the stalls until the comedian had finished his act.

Danny Kaye's fantastic success is part of Palladium folklore, the story most often quoted by the theatre's old hands. The theatre has known many nights of triumph, but none greater than his.

Second Turn: The Comedians

I was at a dinner once and the speaker didn't turn up. They were desperate for someone to make a speech, so they asked me to stand in. I said, 'I can't do that, I wouldn't know what to talk about.' 'Don't worry,' said the chairman, 'you'll think of something.'

So I gave a talk about sex. And it went over sensationally.

Anyway, when I got home my wife asked me how the dinner went, and I told her I had to make a speech. Not wanting to shock her, I said the subject I spoke on was sailing.

The next day the missis is shopping in town and bumps into our bank manager. 'What a marvellous speech your husband gave last night,' he told her. 'It was the best I've ever heard.'

'I can't understand why,' said the wife. 'He doesn't know much about the subject. In fact, he's only done it twice. Once he was sick, and the second time his hat fell off.'

YOU LUCKY PEOPLE!

Second turn on a Variety bill is traditionally reserved for the comic. Tommy Trinder was one of the first to tread this well-worn path to the top. 'I played all the Moss theatres, second turn; twelve minutes, £12' he says. 'We stood in front of a backcloth covered with advertisements. It might depict a street scene. There would be an airship with McDougall's self-raising flour painted on the side; a bus siding extolling the virtues of Ted's Night Powder; and an old man with a sandwich board urging you to eat at Barneys.' There was one snag — the comic had to keep moving about the stage. If he stood in front of an advertisement for too long, the business which had bought the space would refuse to pay for it.

George Black spotted Trinder when, as a brash, aggressive young comedian, he was playing the Birmingham Hippodrome where Hollywood heart-throb Ramon Novarro was topping the bill, trying out his act before making his début at the Palladium. Trinder received a call to London and an appointment with George Black at the Moss Empires offices. Overnight his wages rose from £12 to £35 — and Trinder treated himself to a huge American Oldsmobile on hire purchase. A flash car and a two-year contract were no passport to the Moss Mecca, however. The Crazy Gang were in residence, and it was six years before Trinder saw his name on a Palladium poster, in the show 'Band Waggon'. It opened at the Palladium on 3 July 1939, and Black's assessment of the abrasive cockney comic was confirmed.

When 'Band Waggon' came off, Trinder was booked for a new spectacular, 'Top of the World'. Black spent £36,000 to spirit his audience from blitz-torn London to a fantasy world inhabited only by Amazons. Once Trinder and his co-stars, the Crazy Gang, arrived, the planet's sole preoccupation was learning the art of love.

The revue opened with two lovers, Trinder and Pat Kirkwood, sitting in Hyde Park. A balloon barrage squad — played by the Crazy Gang — anchored their balloon to the couple's bench. A strong wind blew up and wafted away the balloon — and the bench. The scene gave way to a film of the balloon floating higher and higher, with six Lilliputian figures dangling from the sides. The intrepid adventurers landed on a new planet with one earthly possession, a portable radio. They switched it on, and out came the voice of Raymond

Glendenning describing the troubles back home. 'Do you still want to leave?' asked the Amazon Queen. 'Not bloody likely,' said the earthlings.

While Trinder and company were on their dream planet, the Luftwaffe were bombing London. The cast ran a sweepstake on who would walk on stage first after the air raid siren at Marlborough Street police station had sounded the warning. Trinder won. The following night he won again. Finally the truth dawned on the cast. The Germans were working to a clockwork schedule — the raid was planned for exactly the same time every evening. 'That ended my winning run,' muses Trinder.

It was also the end of 'Top of the World'. The capital was under constant bombardment. When the neighbouring Holborn Empire was hit, the Government decided all theatres must close. The curtain came down after just four days — the shortest run in the history of the Palladium.

'We used to climb on the roof to watch the dog fights', says Trinder. 'Half London seemed to be in flames. So much water was being used fighting the fires that the hydraulic system which raised and lowered the safety curtain was constantly breaking down. The curtain would steadily drop lower and lower, and we would have to rush the end before the audience lost sight of us altogether.'

It was six months before the Palladium reopened — without Trinder. But not for long. The following year he was back with Bebe Daniels and Ben Lyon in 'Gangway' — gowns by Norman Hartnell, sketches by Val Guest. It was during the run of this show that Trinder's much-publicised egoncentricity came to the fore. Black told him that a member of the cast had suggested Trinder's name should not be at the top of the bill. 'That's all right,' retorted the comic. 'Take my name off your bill. I'll put my own up.'

He did, too. The Borough Bill Posting Company offered Trinder twenty-six sites for £265 a week. 'Because it was war-time and there was a paper shortage, advertisers were using sheet iron. It cost me more for the iron than it did for the sites!' The hoardings were hand-painted and carried a cartoon of Trinder and a slogan that was to become synonymous with this son of a London tram driver: 'If it's laughter you're after — TRINDER'S the name!' He secured the plum sites, too. A poster went up in Piccadilly Circus, another in Leicester Square. There was even one in Hebrew outside Aldgate Tube station in London's East End.

In Trinder's next Palladium show the orchestra leader wore a dinner jacket with the letters T.R.I.N.D.E.R. emblazoned across the back. Later, Trinder had his own brand of cigarettes made, bigger than the standard brands and each carrying his name embossed in gold.

Trinder's humour was saucy, but never filthy:

> *I hate zip fasteners on trousers. It's like opening a double garage door to get the bike out. I said to the wife, 'Why are you ironing your bra? You've nothing to put in it.' She said, 'I iron your underpants, don't I?'*

His ad-libs with the audience became his stock-in-trade. Night after night he would stick out his ample chin and trade punch-lines with good-humoured hecklers. Servicemen in the war-time audiences bore the brunt of Trinder's attacks. On one occasion a rear admiral walked in after the show had started. 'You're very late, aren't you?' said Trinder. 'Still, you're excused. You had to wait for the tide to come in.'

But another night he met his match. A war film starring Trinder, called *The Bells Go Down*, had just been released. In the film Trinder was killed. When a couple arrived late at the Palladium, Trinder told them, 'This isn't the cinema, you know. You can't stay and see the beginning through again. By the way, if you want to see a good film, go round the corner to the Empire — they're showing one of mine.' 'No thanks,' shouted the latecomer. 'If I'm going to see you die, I'd rather it was at the Palladium.'

Often Trinder would arrive for a matinée still in his pyjamas. 'I figured I had to change when I reached the theatre, anyway, and in those days I could park my car right outside the stage door and make a quick streak in.'

Topping the bill at the Palladium in war-time had its tragic side. Trinder was a close friend of the celebrated plastic surgeon, Sir Archibald McIndoe, whose patients at East Grinstead Hospital were servicemen who had suffered appalling burns and injuries. McIndoe suggested to Trinder that it would be good therapy if one Sunday each month he took the Palladium cast to the hospital and put on a show. Trinder agreed. After the show there would be a dance, with the Palladium showgirls acting as partners to the disfigured soldiers, sailors and airmen. 'They had all the guts in the world, those girls,' remembers Trinder. 'I have seen a girl dance with a wounded serviceman, go outside and vomit, and come back to the floor and continue the dance as if her partner was the most handsome man on earth.'

Yet even in pathos, there was humour. Trinder used to pay for a box at the theatre to be reserved for wounded servicemen, and actress Elizabeth Allen supplied a car to convey them to and from the hospital. On one special occasion, however, the whole area of the stalls was covered with wooden planks so that patients on stretchers, crutches or in wheelchairs could watch the show.

Afterwards a fleet of ambulances and vans lined up in Argyll Street to ferry the troops back to the hospitals. As this was a slow operation, Trinder went on stage and kept the waiting servicemen entertained. Gradually the theatre emptied until just two soldiers were left on the wooden platform.

Trinder continued cracking gags. Still nobody arrived to collect the two soldiers. Exhausted, he finally called out: 'Tell me, how did you two get here?'

'By bus,' one of them replied. 'But the show was so good we didn't want to leave.'

It was Trinder who introduced the Palladium Oscar. 'Have my name done in brass, not on a card,' he told Black. 'I'm not one of those artists who only stays a couple of weeks.'

He was right. The man who starred in the shortest-ever Palladium run was to break all records with 'Happy and Glorious' — a triumphant, flag-waving revue which announced to all that peace was truly on the way. The show ran from October 1944 until the middle of 1946 — 938 glorious performances.

Recently Trinder was back at the Palladium to compère a privately-organised Sunday night concert. 'I didn't know who the promoter was or whether he had the money to pay my fee,' he says. 'But it didn't matter. I'd have done it for nothing, just to get back on that stage.'

> *Now here's a funny thing; now this is a funny thing.*
> *I went home the other night — there's a funny thing.*
> *I went in the back way, through the kitchen, through*
> *the dining-room into the living-room. There's a fellow*
> *standing there, not a stitch on.*
> *Can you imagine that, lady? How's your memory,*
> *gal?*
> *I called the wife in, I said. 'Who's this?' She said,*
> *Don't lose your temper, Miller. Don't go raving mad.*
> *He's a nudist. . .and he's come to use the phone.'*

Trinder's great rival at the London Palladium was the Cheeky Chappie himself, Max Miller. The master of the *double entendre* and the perfectly-timed pause, Miller gained a reputation as a blue comedian. At one time he was banned from the BBC, and a theatre manager once brought the curtain down on him.

Miller, tongue in cheek, insisted he was never vulgar. 'Crack a dirty joke? I never crack a dirty joke. You think I want to get pinched? All my jokes have double meanings; I can't help it if people get the wrong one.'

A parson once wrote to Miller complaining that his daughter had seen the show and been shocked by some of the gags. Miller wrote back saying that the vicar should be ashamed of himself. 'A well-brought-up daughter wouldn't *understand* my jokes.'

'He was the daddy of the repartee merchants,' says Jimmy Jewel; 'The greatest British comic I ever saw,' enthuses Ted Ray. Yet, according to Trinder, although a great performer and wonderful personality on stage, off the boards he lacked one vital quality — a sense of humour.

One night Trinder walked on stage and told the audience:

'I don't know why I'm working so hard, two shows a day, every day. Still, it's not so bad. I'm at the Palladium and Max Miller — ha, ha — he's at the Chelsea Palace.' Miller was furious. Trinder's remark cut deep, for the two comics had enjoyed a pendulum career at the number one Variety theatre. When Trinder's 'Top of the World' was forced to close in September 1940, it was Miller's 'Applesauce' that replaced it when the theatre reopened. When 'Applesauce' ended its run, Trinder was back in 'Gangway'.

Miller contacted his solicitor and a letter was dispatched threatening legal action over Trinder's gag. Unperturbed, Trinder pinned the letter up in the Palladium foyer for all to see, and even wrung a new joke from the situation. He discovered a man who was the double of Miller's agent, Julius Darewski. Every night Trinder would repeat his caustic comment about his rival — to be interrupted by his stooge, dressed in frock coat and top hat, marching down the centre aisle waving an umbrella and shouting: 'I'm Max Miller's agent. I object! I object!'

Miller's trademark was an outlandish garb of florid silk plus-fours, garish silk dressing-gown, dazzling kipper tie, white shoes, and a white trilby set jauntily on one side. For the 1937 Royal Variety Performance at the Palladium he wore a suit of red, white and blue. 'I know how to dress for these occasions,' he said. 'Nice and quiet.'

In the mid-thirties, Miller was topping the bill at the Palladium. The theatre programme carried advertisements for Miller records — which you could buy for 1s 6d — with suggestive titles like "Why Should the Milkman Get it All?', 'Lulu, I Know That You Do' and, probably his most successful, 'Mary from the Dairy', his signature tune. He was reputedly the first British comic to be paid £1,000 a week and spent this vast fortune on such luxuries as a glass-topped Rolls Royce and a six-berth cabin cruiser.

Miller delivered his dialogue at a frenetic pace. Dubious lines were spoken with a roll of his blue eyes, a flicker of the eyebrows and a mischievous glance to the side. He would produce two joke books on stage — one white, the other blue —

and ask the audience to choose which one he should crack his gags from. They always roared back, 'The *blue* one, Max. The blue one!'

Not to be outdone by Trinder's longest run, Miller created a Palladium record himself. For twenty weeks in 1944 he topped the bill in straight Variety, an achievement never bettered at the theatre.

His appearance at the Palladium in the 1950 Royal Variety Performance left less happy memories. Miller was scheduled to do an eight minute spot. Sitting in his dressing-room during rehearsals, he listened to Jack Benny over the Tannoy. 'These Americans get all the time they need,' Max complained, and determined not to do the act he'd rehearsed.

He spent the first half of the show in the bar. When his turn came, he walked on stage carrying a heavily-jewelled mace, held it up to the Royal Box and said, 'I've been to the Tower today, lady. The Crown Jewels will look funny without that lot, won't they? Look, they say there's no money about. Don't believe it. I'm filthy with it. I'm filthy without it, you'll find out.' Miller was soon running well over his allotted time, and the audience was loving it. Producer Charlie Henry was signalling from the prompt corner for him to come off stage. Miller glared at him. 'Don't keep yelling "Come off". I'm on here and I'm going to have a go.'

Miller left the stage to tumultuous applause. Back in the dressing-room he was full of himself — until the door burst open and Val Parnell stormed in. 'Miller,' he roared. 'You'll never work in one of my theatres again.' That night Miller was banished from the line-up of artists presented to the Royal Family. Later Miller's agent Darewski apologised. 'Max had planned to do the blue-book-white-book routine', he explained, 'but when he got on stage and felt for the books, they had disappeared. It was a terrible ordeal for him, especially on that occasion, and he had to act quickly. He decided to put over the act he had been doing for the past few weeks. This went well over the allotted time, but he had to complete it or the act would have been a failure.' Darewski claimed the joke books were still missing. 'They may have been taken by a practical joker,' he said.

It was two years before Parnell forgave Miller and included him on a Palladium variety bill. Just prior to the opening Miller lost his famous cane. Parnell immediately ordered a replacement to be made. Unlike the joke books, the original cane turned up in the nick of time.

Miller suffered a heart attack in 1959 and went into semi-retirement. During one of his last appearances he looked down mischievously at a rotund lady in the audience who was rocking with laughter.

'Go on, laugh, lady,' he said. 'When I've gone there'll never be another.'

The Queen Mother was visiting a hospital one day. As she was walking round the wards she stopped beside a bed and said to the patient, 'Well, my man, what's wrong with you?'

'I've got a boil on me bum, Ma'am.'

The matron was standing nearby and heard what the patient had said. She walked over, very agitated, and said, 'Why did you tell Her Majesty that you had a boil on your bum? Couldn't you have put it a little more politely and said you had a boil somewhere else?'

Well, it so happened, a few weeks later the Queen Mum was visiting the same hospital, and she stopped by the same bed. 'Well, my man,' she said, 'what is wrong with you?'

'I've got a boil on my . . . er, chest, Ma'am.'

'Oh!' said the Queen Mum. 'It's moved has it?'

On 31 March 1974 'Big Hearted' Arthur Askey stood on the Palladium stage to receive the congratulations of a host of show business friends and admirers. It was fifty years to the night since he first trod the boards at the Electric Theatre in Colchester with the Song Salad Concert Party.

His buoyant gait and youthful exuberance made nonsense of his seventy-four years: 'Look at me, no make up — just Polyfilla.' His material has lasted the course pretty well, too.

According to Askey, 'It just goes to prove Abraham Lincoln wrong. You can fool all of the people all of the time.'

Father Bear said, 'Who's been eating my porridge?'
Baby Bear said, 'Who's been eating my porridge?'
Mother Bear said, 'Shut up. I haven't made the bloody porridge yet.'

It was 1939 when Askey got his big break at the Palladium, co-starring with Richard 'Stinker' Murdoch and Tommy Trinder in 'Band Waggon', a show which was based on a popular radio programme of the day. The show had had a chequered career. Launched on radio the previous year, the scripts were so poor that the BBC decided to abandon the project after six broadcasts. Askey and Murdoch protested, and rashly announced that they could turn in funnier material themselves. The Corporation took them up on it and 'Band Waggon' became a national institution. It also gave birth to those familiar Askey catchphrases, 'Hello Playmates', and 'I thank you', and was the forerunner of such radio classics as 'ITMA', 'Take It From Here', and 'Ray's a Laugh'.

Similar teething troubles were to plague the show when it switched to the stage. When Jack Hylton first presented the show in the West End, it flopped. Hasty changes were made. Tommy Trinder was added to the cast and the revamped 'Band Waggon' went on the road at the Palladium on 3 July 1939. Charles Smart played the mighty Compton organ; Bruce Trent provided the vocals; Billy Ternant and his band introduced a new dance sensation — the 'Boomps-a-Daisy'; Arthur Askey sang the 'Bee Song', and a precocious young man called Ernest Wise made his Palladium début as a 'singer and dancer'.

Incredibly, it was not until 1947 that Arthur Askey appeared in Variety at the Palladium, on a bill topped by Vic Damone ('one performer who daren't have his initials on his car number plate'). It was as a pantomime dame that Askey established himself with Palladium audiences. His first dame was a turning point in his long career. It was 1957 and Askey was playing Rhyl, which is outside the number one theatre circuit. 'I thought to myself, hello, the rot is setting in.' The London Palladium seemed a whole world away. The telephone rang: would he like to play 'mum' to David Whitfield and Tommy Cooper in the Palladium panto 'Robinson Crusoe?' The little man was back in the big time.

One of the highspots of that 1957 production was an 'underwater' ballet sequence as Crusoe's ship foundered and sank to the bottom of the ocean. Girls, suspended on wires, created the effect of fish swimming under the sea, and the elevator stage rose to deposit a huge sea shell. Arthur suggested to producer Robert Nesbitt that the scene could finish on a humorous note by having Tommy Cooper descend from the flies dressed in frogman's flippers and snorkel. The idea was tried at rehearsals. Cooper came down on the wire on cue. Suddenly he let out a piercing scream. 'I'm not doing that again,' he yelled. 'That harness was killing me.' Askey explained that while the harness was all right for the girls, a fellow needed to protect himself underneath. 'Wrap some towels between your legs under the swimming trunks,' he told Tommy. Next rehearsal Tommy Cooper was still in agony, but, like a true professional, he was ready to endure pain if it brought a laugh.

On the opening night the moment came for Cooper's 'underwater' entrance. Askey looked up expecting to see his co-star descending on the wire, but he was nowhere to be seen. Instead, from the wings there came a flip-flop, flip-flop sound. Arthur turned — and to his amazement there was Tommy Cooper walking on in flippers.

'Why weren't you on the wire?' he asked when the curtain came down.

'I decided I couldn't go through with it,' said Cooper. 'I'm too fond of children.'

Ten years passed, and 'Robinson Crusoe' returned to the Palladium. This time it was Arthur Askey's turn to be in agony. He fell through a trap door on stage, cracked a couple of ribs and was rushed to the intensive care unit at St. George's Hospital with a heart attack. His lawyers urged him to sue the theatre. 'It was entirely the Palladium's fault and I could have retired to a bungalow in Bournemouth with a fat cheque in my pocket,' he says. 'But I knew that if I took the money I could never work again. I love the business too much. I just couldn't do it.'

Among the traditions of pantomime are the practical jokes — such as filling the dame's shopping bag with heavy weights before 'she' goes on. Singer Mary Hopkin was the butt for one of Askey's tricks in 'Cinderella'. When the moment came for Cinders to try on the crystal slipper, Askey had substituted a Wellington boot. Mary Hopkin spent the entire scene walking around the stage in one boot and one slipper, trying desperately to keep a straight face.

There was a certain justice, then, in Askey's embarrassing moment at the Palladium. He was walking along the corridor backstage when he saw a figure whom he took to be his co-star, Danny La Rue, in drag. Askey went up to him, pinched his bottom and said, 'Wotcher, cock!' His victim wheeled round with a furious exclamation. It was Carol Channing.

For many years Arthur Askey wore a dress suit on stage. At the first rehearsal for 'Band Waggon', Parnell called him aside. 'You aren't going on dressed like that, are you?' he asked. 'This is a music hall, not a concert. If you wear those clothes you'll have the audience laughing at you.'

What more could any comedian ask?

We've got a wonderful show for you tonight, ladies and gentlemen. We've got artists from all four corners of the Labour Exchange.

From Russia we've got the famous sword swallower, Vladimir Kutizheadoff; Ann Twerp from Belgium; there's a chap from Switzerland who will be sitting on his tickling stick and yodelling. We've got the ugliest stripper in the world — the last time she appeared she had the audience shouting 'Get 'em on!' And we've got a yogi who will do the splits over a blow lamp and sing 'Tears'. His name is Singe.

When the Squire of Knotty Ash, Ken Dodd, appeared at the Palladium in September 1974, someone in the audience calculated that he cracked nine hundred jokes in ninety minutes on stage. A few months earlier Doddy had broken the World Joke-Telling Record — previously held by Sammy Davis Jnr. — when he told gags continuously for three hours and six minutes. However, Doddy's record too has since been beaten.

During one Palladium appearance Dodd was in two minds whether or not to crack a string of political jokes. That ebullient character Bessie Braddock, who was Member of Parliament for Liverpool, had brought Harold Wilson to see the show. When Doddy reached the point in his act where he usually went into his Harold Wilson routine, the band in the pit began to laugh. They had laid bets that the Liverpool comic would censor that part of his act for this performance.

Ken Dodd looked down at Mr. Wilson, who was seated six rows back. 'Mr. Wilson,' he said. 'The band are daring me to crack the gags I tell when you're not here. What do you think?'

'You go right ahead, Ken,' said the then Prime Minister.

Harold's just gone into hospital for a little operation. He's going to have his raincoat removed . . . Have you seen him on TV, puffing away at his pipe? Sitting there having his Condor moment . . . He says, 'Vote for me. I'll get you out of the mess the country's in. I've got to — I've got another one round the corner waiting to take its place . . .' Any Americans in? You had a President Wilson, didn't you? Want him back?

Nobody laughed louder than Harold Wilson.

If not exactly the turning point in Ken Dodd's career, his two summer seasons at the Palladium — 'Doddy's Here', in 1965, and 'Doddy's Here Again', in 1967 — went a long way towards establishing him as a national star. Hit records like 'Tears', 'Eight by Ten', and 'Happiness' were in the charts and Doddy was writing a column for the *News of the World*. 'The first time I was offered the Palladium the money was a third of what I was getting on Blackpool Central Pier,' Doddy says. 'When I complained, I was told you do it for the honour. I said: 'Not Ken Dodd, he doesn't. I want the honour — and the money.'' '

50

When he appeared at the Palladium in 1974, Dodd was searching for someone to play his butler, Knocker, whose only duty was to carry Doddy's floor-length moggy coat and Diddy hat off stage after the opening minutes of his act. Louis Benjamin suggested using the theatre's maintenance man, Robert Rudd. A cheery little man, Rudd was only too eager to swap his boiler suit and beret for a butler's white shirt and tails — even if only for a few minutes each night. Unbeknown to the Palladium staff, he had, in fact, appeared in several silent movies. But in his twenty-five years at the Palladium nobody had ever before asked him to appear on the stage.

'The first time I walked on to collect Ken's gear, the hat — being so large — fell right over my face and down to my shoulders,' remembers Rudd. 'When Doddy yanked it off, I said, "Blimey, it ain't 'alf dark in there." The audience laughed, so we kept it in.'

At the end of the show's run, producer Albert Knight assembled the company and crew on stage and presented 'Knocker' with his own brass nameplate — star treatment for one of the back-room boys without whom the show just couldn't go on.

> *Woman goes to the doctors. She says, 'Here, doctor, I haven't been taking my contradictive pills.' Doctor says, 'I beg your pardon?' She says, 'Well, I haven't been taking my contradictive pills.' The doctor says, 'You're ignorant.' She says, 'Yes — three months.'*

'I wanna tell yer a storeeeeeee!' Early in 1950 a young comic from the East End of London was playing the Finsbury Park Empire. The previous week he had appeared at the Glasgow Empire, by reputation a graveyard for comedians. But the young man did well — so well that reports reached the desk of the Moss Empires boss, Val Parnell.

Moss Empires kept a mammoth card index on every artist who ever appeared at any one of their thirty-six halls, compiled from reports sent in by the managers of each theatre.

Each card was sub-divided into sections with a variety of headings; for instance:

Name: Joe Smith.

Theatre: New Cross Empire.

Date: July 1945.

Worth: £45 (or £5; or 'he ought to be paying us money').

Manager's comments: Tolerable (or 'worth persevering with'; or 'a right load of old rubbish').

Should he be booked again? Yes (or 'maybe'; or 'over my dead body').

Even if an artist managed to come through the card test unscathed, there was another hurdle to overcome – the Opposition Book. In this was detailed exactly where the performer was playing when he wasn't appearing at a Moss Theatre. So, even if Joe Smith had once brought the house down at New Cross, playing Lewisham (a rival neighbouring theatre) the week before would immediately disqualify him from another booking.

Cissie Williams, an eccentric lady with a red setter dog called Sandy, was the bookings controller. To her fell the daunting task of making up a Variety bill for each of those thirty-six theatres, fifty-two weeks a year. Without that card index, it is doubtful whether she could ever have completed the task. Cissie would attend the first house each Monday at Finsbury Park, a flask of tea in one hand, packet of sandwiches in the other. Often she would tear a show to pieces. It is said that artists' agents turned away by Cissie without being offered a booking would slip her dog a hefty kick as they went out of her office.

However, back to our young comic. One of the cards in Cissie's tray bore his name, but the rare eulogy from Glasgow had short-circuited the system. Parnell decided to assess the comedian for himself and on Monday night he watched him secretly from the stalls at Finsbury Park. At the end he left without comment.

Ted Ray was on the bill at the Palladium that week. Prior to accepting the booking, Ray had signed to appear at a charity show in Manchester on the Wednesday, and Parnell

Tommy Trinder at the Palladium, 1944

The Cheeky Chappie, Max Miller

Arthur Askey with Sabrina

*Ken Dodd enjoys a joke in his Palladium dressing-room with Mr. and Mrs.
Harold Wilson and Bessie Braddock, 1965*

(Keystor

Max Bygraves meets his audience, 1950

Ted Ray and Val Parnell, 1952

Larry Grayson and his Palladium
'Oscar'

(Doug McKenzie)

Des O'Connor, Billy Dainty and Ron Parry in 'Stars in your Eyes', 1960

needed a stand-in. The young comic's manager, Jock Jacobsen, was in the Moss offices when the dilemma over Wednesday's stand-in was being discussed. 'Why not give the fellow you saw on Monday night a chance?' he suggested, and Parnell agreed.

It meant a hectic day for the young comedian because Wednesday was matinée day at the Palladium. He played the matinée, dashed across to Finsbury Park for the first house, back for the Palladium first house, across to Finsbury Park for the second house and back to the Palladium for his final show. Five performances in under seven hours.

Two months later he was at the Palladium in his own right, billed simply as 'Max Bygraves — comedian'. He was back on the bill for the following week. This time the programme read, 'Retained — Variety's newest comedian'.

Since that first booking as Ted Ray's stand-in, no comedy star has made more appearances at the London Palladium than Max Bygraves.

So many famous comedians have appeared at the Palladium that it is impossible to mention them all. George Mozart assured himself a booking at the Palladium by investing in the syndicate that owned the theatre. But it was his mirth, not his money, that kept him on the Variety bill for thirty-eight consecutive weeks.

Billy Merson, on the other hand, took the Palladium to court because, he claimed, the theatre was working him too hard. Merson — who wrote and first sang 'The Spaniard that Blighted my Life' — was appearing at the theatre when Charles Gulliver decided to switch from two shows a day to three. Merson's contract stipulated that he would play 'any matinée' the management might reasonably desire. The comic argued that a daily afternoon performance was not a matinée. George Robey, the 'Prime Minister of Mirth,' was called to give evidence on the comic's behalf, but to no avail. Merson lost his case.

Scottish actor-comedian Will Fyffe demanded a colossal

£100-a-week fee for his first appearance at the Palladium in 1921. He proved value for money. After six days he was promoted to top of the bill and London, as well as Glasgow, 'belonged to him'. By the 'forties, when George Formby was starring at the Palladium, the artistes' salaries had risen to four figures. Yet Formby made do with five shillings a week pocket money during his stay at the theatre.

Another bill-topping North Country comedian gained a reputation as a theatrical soak and found increasing difficulty in getting bookings. He would plead, 'Look, Guv'nor, lock me in my dressing-room, then I won't be able to visit the pub between shows.' Eric Tann, former musical supervisor for Moss Empires, remembers the comic's appearances vividly: 'During rehearsals he would strike up a friendship with a member of my orchestra and cajole him into taking a bottle of whisky to the dressing-room door each evening. The bandsman would hold the opened bottle against the keyhole, while on the other side of the door the comic sipped merrily away at the contents − through a straw. The subterfuge worked, for he played the Palladium many times.'

It was in 1940 that Jack Warner made his Palladium début. His opening line in those days was not the familiar 'Evenin' all' of 'Dixon of Dock Green', but 'Mind my bike!' Each evening Jack would ruffle his hair, don a dishevelled army uniform and make his entrance through the centre aisle of the stalls on a rusty old bicycle. The show was 'Garrison Theatre', based on a popular radio programme of the same name. Warner's 'Mind my bike', 'My bruvver', and 'Little gel' became national catchphrases − to the extent that one irate father wrote to Jack Warner, 'I agree you have a very successful show, and we all like it. But I must tell you that I have spent hundreds of pounds on my son's education and all he can do now is run round the house shouting in a raucous cockney voice, "Mind my bike". '

There were many emotional nights at the Palladium during 'Garrison Theatre' 's run. 'We built boxes at the side of the stage and filled them with soldiers to give the impression of a real garrison theatre,' Jack Warner recalls. 'Sometimes we had to bring the troops in off the streets. Servicemen lifted from the beaches of Dunkirk in the morning, were on the Palladium stage the same night. Half of them sitting there watching the show thought it was all a dream. The biggest ovation I ever received in my life was the night I went on and announced that our boys had shot down 185 German planes.'

In 1963 a much-loved comic made his come-back at the Palladium. Tony Hancock, son of a Bournemouth hotel-keeper, insisted he was nothing like the television character that had been created for him — the seedy, bombastic, day-dreaming con-man. When 'Hancock's Half Hour' finished on TV, it left a void in small-screen comedy, while Hancock struggled to shake off the East Cheam image.

He was booked to appear at the Talk of the Town but at the eleventh hour cried off. The rumour was that Hancock had lost his nerve for a West End audience. Then fate took a hand. Arthur Haynes was starring with Frank Ifield and Susan Maugham in 'Swing Along' at the Palladium, when he was taken ill. Hancock was available and was offered the spot. Nicholas Parsons introduced him to the audience as 'that delightful character from East Cheam'. But Hancock walked on stage in a snappy three-button suit and insisted, 'This is the new midnight blue Hancock. No more "stone 'em" and "Give 'em a punch in the hooter". Oh no. You're going to get the lot tonight. I'm going through the card.' For the next thirty-seven minutes he did impressions of Nat King Cole, recited Shakespeare, threw in some slapstick and burlesqued the Bolshoi Ballet. The audience liked him, but preferred him in his role as the lad from East Cheam.

In his dressing-room — which still bore Arthur Haynes's name — Hancock sat boxer-like in a blue, yellow and white striped dressing-gown. A red towel was slung around his neck. On the table a celebratory bottle of champagne cooled in the ice bucket. 'It wasn't a new act,' he confessed. 'Just a development of the music-hall turn I did before TV came along. I'm very happy. Yes, very happy — although the act might need a little tightening up.'

In 1968 Tony Hancock took his own life with an overdose of barbiturates washed down with vodka; a poignant reminder that it is not always fun to play the fool.

The comedian Billy Dainty was responsible for a cruel trick on Des O'Connor when they appeared together in the late 'fifties in a show which starred Cliff Richard. O'Connor, Dainty and Ron Parry were billed as 'three up-and-coming young comics'. But although they worked together brilliantly on stage and were the best of friends off, there was still that friendly rivalry that always exists between comedians. After a few weeks it was obvious that the show was destined for a long run. The three youngsters had done so well it was decided that the Palladium Oscar should be extended to these down-the-bill artists and pinned on their dressing-room doors. Dainty waylaid the carpenter and persuaded him to fix the nameplate on Ron Parry's door and his own, but to leave Des O'Connor's for the time being. Later, Dainty and Parry led the backstage procession to see their coveted Oscars. O'Connor stood in a corner, a little sheepishly. 'They don't seem to have got round to putting my nameplate up yet,' he said dejectedly. 'Well, the carpenter probably hasn't had the time,' he was assured.

Several days passed and still no Oscar appeared on Des O'Connor's door. The stage hands were party to the joke and feigned astonishment whenever he tackled them about the missing trophy. Finally, he could stand it no longer and confronted Dainty.

'I'm sorry, Des,' said Billy, 'but I've heard a rumour that only two of us are being kept on. They didn't say who the unlucky one was to be.'

Des O'Connor was convinced he was out of the show. It was more with relief than anger that he learned the truth.

Billy Dainty opened in another Palladium show the night after his son was born. But there were complications. The baby weighed only three and a half pounds and was not expected to live. 'I was absolutely shattered,' says Dainty. 'I went on at the Palladium on Monday night without the foggiest idea of what I was doing. To this day I cannot remember a thing about that performance.' So distracted was Dainty that when he left the theatre he jumped into a parked Rolls Royce instead of his modest little car. Next morning, he read the reviews of the show. One critic wrote, 'Last night Variety returned to the Palladium. Joe Church came on and showed us why Variety is still very much alive. Then Billy Dainty came on and showed us why it almost died.'

A few nights later he was told the baby would live. 'I went on stage and knocked 'em for six,' Dainty remembers. As he walked off, one of the stage hands stopped him: 'Blimey,' he said, 'what happened? I'd never have recognised you as the fellow who opened on Monday night.'

Harry Secombe is always top of the bill as far as the backstage staff at the Palladium are concerned. Not only is he as warm and friendly off-stage as he appears on, but his regular backstage parties ('Harry's Happies') and the ever-open door of his dressing-room ('Harry's Bar'), have helped cement a firm relationship between artist and crew.

Secombe's first Palladium appearance was in 1956, when he topped the bill in a revue called 'Rocking the Town.' His only previous West End engagement had been ten years before as a £20-a-week comic turn between the nudes at the Windmill Theatre. But his big 'break' came before he set foot on the Palladium stage. Before rehearsals began, Secombe took a holiday in Bermuda, where the sixteen-stone Goon fell off a rock and broke his arm. From hospital he telephoned Bernard Delfont, the presenter of 'Rocking the Town'. Delfont let out a strangled cry. 'Is it bad?' he asked. 'Can you work?' 'I think so,' Secombe replied.

He was in agony throughout rehearsals, but the show opened on schedule. The broken arm gave him a heaven-sent opening line. 'It's always been my ambition to appear at the Palladium with a large supporting cast,' he said, pointing to his plastered arm.

In another Palladium revue, one of Secombe's entrances was on a stagecoach from which he sang 'If I Ruled the World', the hit song from his previous West End musical 'Pickwick'. One night he was engaged in one of his favourite pastimes — Indian arm wrestling with the backstage crew — when he heard the cue music strike up. He dashed on stage just in time to board the stagecoach as it rolled onto the set, but the arm wrestling had left him so out of breath he was unable to sing a note. 'The band played, and I just *spoke* the words,' he says.

When his coloured co-star in another show was ill one night, Secombe walked on stage to apologise to the audience. 'I'm sorry,' he said, 'but Winifred Atwell won't be with us tonight. She's a bit off-colour'. The audience roared with laughter, while an embarrassed Secombe had a fit of giggles.

The England Test Team paid Secombe a visit the evening before they were to go to Australia to contest the Ashes. The star dressing-room at the Palladium is a double room — one section being a reception lounge and the other the actual dressing area. Each has a separate door. After a few drinks in the reception room, the England skipper Peter May looked at his watch and said, 'Come on, lads, time to go. We've a boat to catch in the morning.' As he led the procession of players out through one door, the other door opened, and Freddie Trueman and Godfrey Evans sneaked back in. 'I hate to think in what condition they arrived at the ship next morning,' says Secombe.

Secombe is never short of friends when he appears at the Palladium. Richard Burton, Geraint Evans and Donald Houston have all sunk a few scotches in 'Little Abergavenny', as the dressing-room is known when the Welsh clan get together. However, one evening there was a Welshman Secombe was not expecting. He arrived at the stage door, said he was Mr. Jones from Swansea, and that he was an old friend of the comedian. Harry was dubious, but went to the stage door to meet the fellow.

'Mr. Secombe,' the man began, 'or may I call you Harry? I resorted to a stratagem to get you out. I've never set eyes on you before but, of course, I know all about you. All I want to say is: *thank you* for holding the audiences of London in the palm of your hand. *Thank you* for keeping the Welsh dragon flying over the West End. *Thank you* for making

Wales a better place for entertainment, and *thank you* for putting Welsh entertainers on the map.'

'Thank you,' murmured Secombe, feeling this response seemed rather less than adequate to the Welshman's glowing tribute.

'Well,' his visitor went on, 'I can't stand here chatting. I'm up here with a convention of civil servants from South Wales. Now — what's the chance of thirty complimentary tickets for second house?'

The Speciality Acts

In the heyday of music hall and Variety, a spot was always reserved on the bill for what was loosely referred to in the profession as the 'speciality act'. Today we are used to the star of a show closing a Variety bill. But almost until the Second World War, that spot was filled by a juggler, wire-walker, acrobat, trampoline artist, contortionist, escapologist, or any other weird and wonderful turn that did not fall neatly into a defined category of show business. They were a motley breed of entertainers, resigned to the fact that the audience had paid their money to see the big names on the bill, and that people often had to leave in the middle of their performance to catch the last bus home. However, they could always take comfort from the knowledge that their eccentric skills were likely to keep them in regular employment long after many of the better-known stars had faded from the scene.

George Carl is one of the most successful members of this dying breed. Like so many of his predecessors, he learned his trade in a circus ring. As a scrawny lad of ten, he left his parents' farm in Michigan, USA, to join a travelling circus where he quickly became adept at acrobatics, the highlight of his performance being a breathtaking somersault from a spring-board over the backs of *five* elephants. He made the transition to Variety and appeared many times at New York's equivalent of the Palladium, the Radio City Music Hall. He was a guest on Ed Sullivan's television show, and was retained for twenty-three weeks. Yet despite his popularity in the States, Carl was unknown in Europe until he appeared at the Crazy Horse night club in Paris in June 1973. There he was spotted as perfect Palladium material and signed up for a short Variety season with Larry Grayson and Noele Gordon. Carl so delighted the audiences that Sir Bernard Delfont invited him to appear in the 1974 Royal Variety Performance.

Describing any speciality act is difficult; describing Carl's is near-impossible. To say he juggles with a hat, ties himself up in a microphone lead, disintegrates a harmonica and wrestles to free his fingers and thumbs from the button-holes of his suit, in no way does justice to his skills. Yet, in a nutshell, that is Carl's act — save for the climax in which he visibly shrinks from his normal 5 feet 2 inches to a midget 2 feet 6 inches.

'It took me twelve years to develop my act,' says Carl. 'I used to be a stand-up comic, but there was so much competition. One night I slotted in my funny walk' — he hot-foots it around the stage steadily getting shorter and shorter, his legs disappearing somewhere in his baggy trousers — 'and I was a hit. Gradually I became more of a mimic and clown and less of a comic, until I found myself going through the entire act without uttering a word.'

He once brought traffic on the Champs Elysées screeching to a halt when he performed his shrinking routine while crossing the busy boulevard. 'I figured the only people French drivers stop for are drunks, idiots and cripples. You have to be a little crazy to do an act like mine.'

'A little crazy' — an apt description. Who in his right mind would twice nightly allow flaming knives to be thrown within an inch of his anatomy; climb barefoot on a ladder of well-honed swords; be bound in chains and plunged into a tank of water; springboard his way to the top of an eighteen-foot pyramid; or balance at the apex of a long, spindly pole?

No speciality act was more bizarre than that performed by The Great Magnet, whose posters proclaimed 'Cannibalism —

see a man eaten alive this Friday.' Naturally this always assured him a full house, particularly as his claim was backed up by a promise to donate five hundred guineas to charity should he fail. The curtains would part to reveal a surgical trolley, a nurse in uniform, and The Great Magnet dressed in surgeon's gown and cap. Not surprisingly, he often had to abandon his proposed meal because of a chronic shortage of volunteers, but when someone was daft — or drunk — enough to volunteer, The Great Magnet would go through a pre-operation ritual of washing his hands, selecting a scalpel — and brushing his teeth. After this, few had the stomach to remain on the operating table. In case they did, The Great Magnet had an ace up his sleeve. He would make a small incision in the victim's arm and dab lysol into the wound. The 'patient' would be in such agony from the disinfectant's sting that he would run screaming from the stage.

Less macabre, but no less eccentric, was Kardomah, who filled the stage with flags of all the nations — hundreds of them, magically produced from sleeves, collar, shirt-front, trouser legs — until the flags filled not only the stage, but the orchestra pit as well. That was his entire act. The hardest part was gathering up the flags and bunting afterwards.

The most famous — and most mimicked — speciality act was Wilson, Keppel and Betty. An American team, they first appeared in Britain at the London Palladium in 1932, and for twenty-five years they remained a top attraction at all the major British Variety theatres. Wilson, Keppel and Betty were 'sand dancers'. Over the years their act changed hardly at all. Jack Wilson and Joe Keppel were two skinny men in T-shirts, skirts, sand shoes and fez; Betty wore a bikini top, cutaway skirt and Cleopatra head-dress.

All three were yoga fanatics, and it was not unusual to see Wilson and Keppel standing on their heads in their dressing-room, which they had adapted into a theatrical workshop. They possessed every conceivable carpenter's tool, and whiled away the hours between shows making their own props, such as staffs, spears and shields. They also spent much of their spare time working on their 'sand carpet' — a large wooden tray with raised edges to keep the sand from littering the stage. After each performance they meticulously sifted the sand to remove any particles of dirt deposited during their dance. So fastidious were they that when the act was booked for Las Vegas, they took their own sand.

The Six Mannelli Girls were a popular act at the Palladium in the 'twenties. The programme notes waxed poetic: 'The six ladies will perform the most difficult feats imaginable with the utmost sang-froid. There is not the slightest doubt that some of the tricks attempted are bordering on the impossible.' The girls' speciality was, in fact, constructing a human pyramid. With such a build-up, one can but hope the pyramid did not collapse on the opening night.

Reading the descriptions of some of the early speciality acts, one can only marvel at the ingenuity of the men and women who devised them: characters like Langston, a German who hung suspended from a wire upside-down over the orchestra pit, and took rifle shots at balloons at the back of the stage: and Chung Ling Soo, from America, whose trick was to catch in a plate a bullet fired from a gun by his assistant. At the Wood Green Empire in 1913 the trick went wrong, and Chung Ling Soo (his real name was William Robinson) was killed. Whether his death was an accident or suicide has remained one of the great theatre mysteries. Then there was Babbette, a drag artist who balanced on a high wire — the only balancing act ever to top a Palladium bill. Most of the audience went home believing the wire-walker really was a woman, for Babbette never removed his wig. The Topsy Turvy Five tap-danced standing on their heads. Impossible? Not if you suspend a tap-board on wires from the flies! Teddy Brown weighed twenty-six stones and played the xylophone. Though a brilliant exponent of the instrument, he could never have matched the feat of a modern-day counterpart, one of a duo called The Mistins, who plays the xylophone while being spun round at a frenetic pace on a pair of roller skates.

In 'Garrison Theatre' the world champion Joe Davis gave a demonstration of snooker, while Charlie Aberdonian spoke the commentary. The snooker table was on castors, and a huge mirror, 24 feet by 4 feet, hung behind it so those in the stalls could see the shots. Playing a snooker game to a Variety bill schedule is not easy. The first occasion Joe Davis tried out his act, he over-ran by seventeen minutes.

In 1944 the world table tennis champion Victor Barna and another leading player, Alec Brook, played a match on the Palladium stage. Seven years later, when Red Skelton topped the bill, a similar game was arranged between Bergmann and Boros.

One of the unlikeliest acts to appear at the Palladium featured Jon Hall, one of a long line of screen Tarzans, who for two weeks in August 1949 filled the famous auditorium with the familiar chest-beating call as he swung across the stage in a loincloth. Then there was glamorous strong-girl Joan Rhodes, whose speciality was ripping up telephone directories, and Terri Carol who practised the gentler art of tearing paper into pretty shapes.

In the early 'thirties there was the Texas Cowboy Band featuring the Champion Rope Thrower of the World — a Captain Tom Hickman. In September 1938 another cowboy star breezed in. His name was Tom Mix, and as in all good Westerns, even this legendary hero of the screen had to hand over his shooting irons to the 'sheriff'. Customs men confiscated eight six-shooters and five rifles which they discovered in the cowboy's luggage.

Tom Mix's Wonder Horse Tony was only one of a whole menagerie of animals to enjoy board and lodging at the Palladium. The pantomime of 1951, 'Humpty Dumpty', boasted the oldest performer ever to appear at the theatre — a centenarian cockatoo. This veteran of the halls had been in show business for ninety-three years. Olsen's Sea Lions were a great favourite in the 'thirties, and earlier still there was Captain Woodward and his performing seals, each one of which played a musical instrument — drum, xylophone, horn and trumpet. Then there was Tanya, an elephant who gained the distinction of appearing in a Royal Variety Performance. Just before the show, her owner Jenda Smaha noticed that she seemed somewhat off-colour. He suspected Tanya might have caught a chill, and disappeared across the road to the nearest public house. When he returned he was carrying a bottle of brandy. Tanya grabbed the bottle and downed the lot. Never did an elephant give a more relaxed performance.

It is not unknown, of course, for a performer to require some Dutch courage before facing an audience. A chimpanzee called Candy appearing in 'Rocking the Town' refused to go on each night until she was offered a drink from Harry Secombe's cocktail cabinet. Luckily for him, Candy was happy to settle for a bottle of Coke.

In most people's eyes, chimpanzees are lovable creatures but the very mention of the species was likely to provoke a few choice expletives from 'Monsewer' Eddie Gray of the Crazy Gang fame. The animals became anathema to him after an incident during a Palladium show in the 'thirties. Whilst one chimp was performing on stage, its partner would be sitting quietly in its stall, waiting its turn to go on. One night, a stick appeared mysteriously through a hole in the stage. The chimpanzee in the stall was bemused. The stick rose higher and higher, then disappeared back through the hole. The chimp went on, performed his trick, and returned to his stall. Again, the stick popped up through the hole. The inquisitive animal made a grab for the stick, but it eluded him and slipped back through the hole. Each time the stick reappeared, the chimp became more and more infuriated. When he could contain his curiosity no longer, he peered into the hole. Pouff! Into the chimp's eye shot a puff of white powder. He was mad with rage.

It was a Crazy Gang practical joke, but the hapless chimp could not see the funny side of it and was determined to vent his wrath on someone. As it happened, that someone turned out to be Eddie Gray, for at that moment, the comedian was walking unsuspectingly on stage to perform his act. The chimp leapt up and down, snarling furiously, and charged towards Gray. Sensing danger, Eddie Gray did a quick circuit of the stage and jumped into the safety of the orchestra pit. He got such a laugh that the Crazy Gang were tempted to keep the joke going every night. But Gray had other ideas. Years later, when the Crazy Gang were searching for an animal act for their show at the Victoria Palace, Eddie insisted on a clause being written into his contract. It said simply: 'Definitely no chimps!'

An early Palladium show called 'Mexico', written by circus owner Albert Hengler and based on the adventures of a fictional hero of the day called Nick Carter, featured a thrilling chase on horseback. The chase ended at the edge of a great lake, represented on stage by a huge tank of water. Around the tank were imitation cliffs made of papier maché. Each night the villain would make his escape by riding to the edge of the cliffs and plunging, with his horse, into the water. The spectacle brought gasps from the audience – and a soaking for the band.

A terrifying speciality act was included in the first Palladium show to feature Flanagan and Allen, in 1931. It was a giant brontosaurus which picked up a girl dancer from the stage and dangled her perilously high above the heads of the audience. As the girl swayed back and forth, the creature snorted steam and fire.

However, it was a dinosaur that Palladium property master Ron Harris tangled with. The monster was built for a space-age revue called 'Man in the Moon', starring Charlie Drake. It was twenty-two feet long and moved across the stage on rails, guided by Harris and his assistant, who were locked away inside its belly. 'One night the bolts holding the sections together jammed,' says Harris. 'We sat roasting like Jonah in the whale for an hour before anybody was able to free us.'

Being stuck inside a prehistoric monster was nothing to the humiliation suffered by one magician at the Palladium. One of his tricks was to make his cane disappear. It was a baffling but simple illusion; before his act the magician would slip his cane into a thin paper sheath painted to resemble the cane. On stage he would tap the cane on the boards to demonstrate to the audience that it was solid, walk a couple of paces, tap the cane again and, hey presto, scoop it up into his hands and make it disappear. What the audience didn't know was that earlier, the magician had drilled a small hole in the stage just wide enough to take the cane. When he tapped the cane the second time, the solid section slid down into the hole, leaving him with the paper-thin sheath which the magician skilfully screwed up and palmed. He had been performing the trick for years and it was going well that week — until maintenance day, that is. The Palladium prides itself on its efficiency, and in those days a stage hand would inspect the floor each week and repair any blemishes that scarred the beloved boards. Naturally, when he spotted the offending hole he plugged it with an old chair leg, sanded the board, and left the stage as good as new.

The magician went on that night. 'Ladies and gentlemen, the disappearing cane!' Tap. . . two paces. . . tap. . .

It is one Palladium story that needs no ending.

My Fair Ladies

Wednesday afternoon at the London Palladium – matinée time. Two women stand in the spotlight, one with flaming red hair, the other older, her hair turned to grey.

The younger woman is a familiar enough show business figure. She has been topping Variety bills for years, made a name for herself in movies, and sold countless thousands of records. The older lady has sung merely for pleasure. Her lifelong ambition to be an actress has never been fulfilled. Yet here she stands on the most famous Variety stage in the world – carving herself a tiny niche in music-hall history.

Her name never appeared in a theatre programme. Had it done, the billing might have read, 'Only on Wednesdays'. For that was the only day of the week Mrs. Sarah Stansfield ever appeared. The redhead was her daughter, Gracie Fields. The Wednesday ritual started one afternoon at the Palladium when Gracie was topping the bill. Her mother sang 'Silver Threads Among the Gold', the audience loved it and, from then on, wherever Gracie appeared on matinée afternoons, Mrs. Stansfield sang a solo, too.

But this Wednesday was different. As Gracie made her customary introduction and the band turned their music to 'Silver Threads. . .', Mrs. Stansfield walked to the microphone and announced, 'I'm not singing that today. I want to launch a newcomer into show business — my grandson, Michael Stansfield.'

Gracie was as surprised as the audience when her young nephew stepped up to the microphone and sang 'Some Enchanted Evening'. His grandmother stood beside the piano, smiling broadly. Suddenly the smile vanished, her face turned ashen, and she staggered back against the piano. Momentarily, she gasped for breath. It was a heart attack. Only a mild one — and it passed in seconds — but Gracie spotted it. A week later Sarah Stansfield was dead.

'I'm convinced she "died" on the Palladium stage,' says Gracie. 'She was so proud of Michael, and she composed herself so quickly that few people in the audience noticed that anything was wrong.'

Gracie Fields is still one of the best loved and most talked-about performers to have appeared at the Palladium. The theatre staff remember the day she spotted an elderly cleaning lady struggling along the centre aisle with a heavy bucket of water. 'Come on, luv,' said Gracie. 'Let me take that.' They talk about the flowers she sent to the Palladium chef when he was taken ill; her generosity when he died; and the signed photographs she posted off to the staff when they wrote to say thank you.

Gracie Fields sang three types of songs: soft, sentimental ballads like 'Little Old Lady', 'Some Day My Prince Will Come' and 'Sally'; the rousing marching tunes featured in her films such as 'Sing As We Go' and 'Wish Me Luck As You Wave Me Goodbye'; and comic ditties like 'Get Me to the Altar, Walter', 'In Me 'Oroscope' and 'The Biggest Aspidistra in the World', sung with a catch in the voice.

Occasionally during a comedy routine, playing a charlady, she would break into something out of Verdi or Puccini while scrubbing away at the floor. Many of her admirers believe she could have had an equally successful career in opera, and the 1952 Royal Variety Performance at the Palladium seemed to present an ideal opportunity to demonstrate her operatic prowess. She was asked to sing a duet with the legendary

Beniamino Gigli. Appropriately they selected 'Come Back to Sorrento'. For a while the Italian tenor dutifully held himself in check to allow Gracie's voice to be heard, then — fortissimo! — the full force of his powerful voice blasted out. Gracie turned her head and glared at him. Gigli turned — and winked.

After the show the dressing-rooms were rife with rumours that Gracie was furious with her singing partner for trying to drown her. Newspapers reported that Gracie had called Gigli 'a villain', but Gracie laughed. 'We were just playing,' she said.

She rehearsed for another Royal Show at the Palladium with a nagging pain in the head. When she mentioned it to a friend he noticed a red spot on her forehead and advised her to see a doctor. Gracie agreed to see a specialist, expecting merely a diagnosis. 'Before I had a chance to object, I was on the couch, under a local anaesthetic and having my forehead cut open.' She came round to discover a great plaster stuck across the top of her face. 'What have you done?' she bellowed at the doctor. 'I've got a Command Performance tonight, I can't appear before the Royal Family looking like this!' The specialist advised her to restyle her hair so that the fringe covered the plaster. 'Nobody will notice,' he assured her. He was right. To this day, Gracie wears her hair to cover that scar.

The lass from the cotton mills of Rochdale in Lancashire was topping the bill at the Palladium in the 'thirties. But it was after the war that she scored her greatest success. Gracie had married her second husband, Monty Banks, an Italian film director, just before the war, and on the outbreak of hostilities he left England as an 'enemy alien'. Not unnaturally, his wife went with him. Her action was misunderstood by many people in Britain, and when she set up home in the United States she was maliciously accused of taking money and jewellery out of the country with her.

In 1948 she returned and met Val Parnell. The Palladium boss had just introduced his American superstar policy at the theatre, but he told Gracie he would be happy to make an exception if it meant her name appearing on the bill. Gracie was hesitant. To help persuade her, Parnell invited her to share a box with him one Saturday night. Just before the inter-mission, female impressionist Florence Desmond — who mimicked Gracie Fields so brilliantly — pointed up to the box, and introduced Britain's long-lost daughter. In the stalls, circle and gallery, they rose as one. Gracie stood to acknow-ledge the cheers — and the theatre resounded to the strains of 'Sally'.

Gracie was convinced. She agreed to close that first glittering Parnell Variety season. Ella Fitzgerald shared the billing, and, fittingly, Florence Desmond was in the show, too.

It was an emotional comeback. Harsh words had been written and spoken about the absent star. Critics had claimed that Gracie was afraid to face a British audience again. Today she dismisses these allegations as poppycock. 'Everyone forgets that I came back to Britain in 1941 and 1943 to tour the factories and forces' camps. The factory girls were marvellous. They never believed that I deserted them.'

Gracie and her third husband, Boris Alperovici, live in a converted fort on Capri. Tourists flock there, amongst them a woman who was just seventeen when she first saw Gracie Fields at the Palladium. 'Now she has four daughters,' says Gracie. 'The eldest is named after me, and every year they all come to Capri for their holiday.'

Proof that 'Our Gracie' will never be forgotten.

July 1974 saw the first appearance at the Palladium of the American pop singer Mama Cass Elliott.

On her opening night she caused a sensation. In 1967, while touring Britain with the Mamas and Papas group, she had been arrested and accused of stealing two blankets and two keys from a London service flat. When she appeared before the Bench, the prosecution had offered no evidence, and the charges were dropped. Now, at the Palladium, she interrupted her songs to confess that she had, indeed, stolen the items. 'Who hasn't taken a souvenir from a hotel some-time?' she asked. That night she further confided in her audience about her weight problem. 'When you get to my age' — she was 33 — 'nasty words like heart attack crop up. It's really not a very nice prospect, so you've got to do something to keep your weight down.' She had tried a number of diets. She had even considered a revolutionary 'by-pass' operation in which food is re-routed through the body so that only sufficient is absorbed to keep the person alive.

The reaction of the audience that first night, and successive nights, was beyond her wildest dreams. They stood and they cheered — unaware of the strain that each performance was placing on the fourteen-stone singer. After each show she slumped exhausted on the couch in her dressing-room. Her days were spent not in the usual round of personal appearances and Press and television interviews, but resting in her Mayfair flat.

So successful was her Palladium fortnight that on the Sunday night following her final performance, Hollywood writer Jack Martin threw a party in her honour. Cass Elliott drank only soda water and nibbled at cheese. She left early, before many of the guests had arrived, still tired after a birthday party for Mick Jagger which she had attended the previous evening.

On the Monday morning her secretary knocked on her bedroom door. There was no answer. The girl went in — and discovered Mama Cass lying dead in bed, naked, with a ham sandwich at her side. At first it was thought she had choked on the sandwich, but a subsequent inquest decided death was due to a heart attack brought on by the singer's obesity.

Before leaving the Palladium on the Saturday night, Mama Cass had scribbled a note in the dressing-room mirror for Debbie Reynolds, who was to follow her at the theatre. The message said simply, 'If the audience are as nice to you as they have been to me, you'll have a wonderful time.'

On Monday Debbie Reynolds was on stage rehearsing when the news broke that Cass Elliott was dead. It was decided that it must be kept from Debbie — it was her first time at the Palladium and nothing must be allowed to upset her. But despite the precautions taken backstage, the news leaked through. Debbie walked slowly and sadly to her dressing-room. The message, in blue make-up chalk, was still on the mirror.

Debbie Reynolds had a battle of her own to fight each night before stepping out on the Palladium stage. Ten days before she was due to leave for London, the diminutive star of films like *The Tender Trap*, *Singin' in the Rain* and *Tammy*, fell while dancing in her cabaret act in a Reno night club. Doctors said her ankle would have to be put in plaster, and she would be unable to dance for six weeks. Debbie insisted she was not going to London with her foot in plaster. 'Can you imagine my being pushed onto the Palladium stage in a wheelchair?' Though she had her way, her ankle was giving her considerable pain. Every day she visited a specialist who massaged her foot and gave her a prescription to relieve a blood clot.

The girl-next-door image Hollywood had created for her had carried Debbie successfully through forty major motion pictures. But the question the London theatre world was asking was, 'What is she going to do when she gets on stage?'

'Well, I'm sure enough not going to stand here for seventy-five minutes singing "Tammy",' she assured her first-night audience. She had brought her entire Las Vegas production to London — not for a long time had the Palladium stage glittered so brightly. She made an extravagant entrance perched on a float of white lights which descended from the flies and spelt out her name. She sang numbers from her hit show, 'Irene'; donned a wardrobe of costumes ranging from a yellow cat-suit to frilly, heavy-skirted party dresses; gave fair impressions of Zsa Zsa Gabor and Mae West, and a devastatingly cruel one of Barbra Streisand (complete with false nose and chewing gum), and completed the extravaganza on a giant staircase with a Fred Astair-Ginger Rogers dance routine.

'I had to fake some of the steps because of my ankle,' says Debbie. 'But only a pro would have noticed.'

Like Mama Cass, she spent her days resting after the exertions of the previous night. Few people realised how close she had come to calling off her Palladium season. However, if she nursed any doubts about the wisdom of completing her engagement, the reaction of the first-night critics quickly dispelled them. They were ecstatic. The London *Evening News,* wrote, 'The Palladium prays for that kind of happening.' The *Daily Express* enthused, 'We saw a delightful talent which her Pollyanna film roles never allowed her to indicate.'

Debbie Reynolds is not the only Palladium leading lady to triumph over adversity at the famous theatre. Shirley Bassey's appearances have a reputation for being somewhat traumatic. 'She is a perfectionist, and that means nothing is too good for her,' says one stage hand. 'Standing up there and doing an emotional striptease is no picnic. There are times when the Palladium stage can be the loneliest place on earth. Most people couldn't do it if you paid them a million pounds.'

Producer Albert Locke recalls one Shirley Bassey performance in particular. The girl from Tiger Bay was excited about a new dress she had bought for a television show being recorded from the Palladium. 'It's gorgeous, clinging and made of lamé,' she told him. But when she stepped on stage at rehearsals, her dress was as dazzling as a car's headlamps to the television cameras. An alternative dress was offered by the wardrobe department, one that the singer had worn before on television. 'I'm not going on in that,' Shirley shouted. Albert Locke had a suggestion. The sheen from an orchestra's instruments often presents a similar problem for the television camreas, so the instruments are sprayed with an antiglare fluid. Why not spray Shirley's dress? To suggest this took some courage – the dress had cost £700. Reluctantly, Shirley agreed. The first spraying had little effect. Neither did the second. There was no turning back now. 'Give it a third coat,' said Locke. Finally the camera crews agreed it would do. The dress clung like a second skin, but she wore it for the recording and gave one of her finest performances – though there isn't much doubt that the dress was ruined.

'Forces Sweetheart' Vera Lynn was another Palladium star with dress trouble. Like Shirley Bassey, she had bought a beautiful new outfit for her appearance. But when she opened her wardrobe on the night of the show, the dress had vanished. Vera stopped off on her way to the theatre and bought a replacement from a Bond Street store. The only snag was, the dress needed altering. The store promised to deliver the re-fitted dress to the Palladium on time. They did. But what the audience — which included royalty — did not know was that Vera Lynn's dress was totally held together by pins throughout her performance.

If Oscars were awarded for perseverance, two Palladium leading ladies would certainly qualify for them.

The first was Nora Bayes, a popular American singing star of the early part of the century. A powerful contralto who had no need of a microphone and possessed a total command of the stage, Nora was a flamboyant character. Her gimmick was a huge ostrich feather fan which she changed each night to match the colour of her dress. She claimed to need £300 a week to live; had five husbands, but no children. On Broadway, a theatre was named after her.

Her first two visits to Britain were miserable flops. In 1923 she returned to play the Coliseum for Sir Oswald Stoll, but again her performance was disappointing. She was booked to appear at the Palladium for a month in the July of that year. Again, the reception from the audience was lukewarm. But so determined was Nora Bayes to prove her talent to British audiences that she made an offer unprecedented on the English stage. 'Continue my engagement indefinitely and I'll accept smaller billing, change my songs every week — and take half salary,' she told Palladium Guv'nor Charles Gulliver. Taken aback, Gulliver agreed and Nora was relegated to a small spot in the first half of the bill.

No longer feeling that the success of the show rested on her shoulders alone, Nora relaxed, grew in confidence and steadily won round the audiences. She introduced new songs every week; but it was not long before the Palladium regulars were shouting for her to repeat her songs of the previous weeks. After six weeks Nora was back on full salary. After ten, her name was restored to the top of the posters.

No less dramatic was the battle for recognition by Britain's

Dorothy Squires. In the 'forties you could hardly switch on the radio without hearing her belting out a Billy Reid composition. Yet it was as a stand-in for 'Two Ton' Tessie O'Shea that Dorothy Squires made her début at the Palladium in 1946. Her career prospered, and when she married a handsome young actor named Roger Moore, romantics dubbed it the perfect love match. But the world began to turn sour for Dorothy Squires in 1961. She and Moore parted, and when she tried to pick up the threads of an interrupted career, it seemed that the entrepreneurs of the entertainment business no longer wanted to know.

Bitterly resentful, she fought a vociferous, and often public, battle with the establishment. She was seen on television only once in nine years — and then she was introduced as rival singer Rosemary Squires. She was invited to appear on 'Top of the Pops', but was then told that as her record had slipped to number 37 in the charts, she was no longer in the show.

Nevertheless, the 'seventies began on a high note. Three records that seemed at least partly autobiographical climbed into the charts — 'For Once in My Life', 'Till' and 'My Way'. She called a press conference and announced, 'I'm going to hire the London Palladium and star in my own show.' The entertainment industry shook its head in sheer disbelief. Mockers christened the project 'Losers Anonymous', and suggested that the performance was merely a costly balm for a bruised ego. Costly it certainly was: £1,000 for hiring the theatre, £1,245 for a 31-piece orchestra, £675 for the arranger and conductor, £675 for a pianist, supporting acts and advertising. 'She is making the biggest mistake she's ever made in a life which has been filled with mistakes,' wrote columnist Lynda Lee-Potter. 'She is laying herself open to defeat, derision and a public humiliation of such magnitude she'll never get over it. Years ago audiences queued for hours to see her. She didn't have to hire a theatre and give away tickets, which is something she is in danger of having to do this time.'

Within two days of Dorothy Squires's announcement, those

words had a hollow ring. The box office was besieged and every seat sold. On the black market £2 seats fetched four times that amount.

On Sunday, 6 December 1970, Dorothy Squires stepped onto the Palladium stage to a standing ovation that lasted a full five minutes. There were shades of Danny Kaye twenty-eight years before as she asked the audience, 'Are you as nervous as I am?'

Dorothy was on stage for ninety minutes. She walked off to an avalanche of flowers and another standing ovation. In her dressing-room she opened the many good luck telegrams, including one from Roger Moore and another offering her two weeks' work in Las Vegas. 'If I never walk on stage again, tonight will have been worth it,' she said. Then she went home to throw a party that lasted until dawn.

Dorothy Squires proved her point — but still she failed to convince the show business moguls. Twice more she hired the Palladium, and then made even that gamble seem a mere bob-each-way flutter by hiring the Carnegie Hall in New York.

Back home again she did the rounds of clubs and cabaret dates, but the West End and television were still taboo. Taboo, that is, until the summer of 1974. Her agent broke the news: 'The Palladium want you to star for two weeks in Variety — and this time Moss Empires are going to foot the bill!'

On a Monday morning in March 1957 the Palladium made headlines in the national newspapers. 'Down comes the curtain as Pearl Bailey climbs about stage,' screamed the banners. 'Singing star who surprised television viewers is very, very sick!' The *Daily Express* reporter began his story: 'Startled television viewers last night saw coloured singing star Pearl Bailey climb down from the Palladium stage into the stalls. Bandsmen moved quickly to help her. Trailing a hand microphone lead, she weaved slowly along the front row, singing snatches of songs in a strained voice. For seven muddled minutes over time, she gallantly ad-libbed through her un-rehearsed excursion off-stage. Still the cameras were kept on her. In the audience there were bewildered murmurs. Finally she reached the side and clambered up on the stage, hauling a man from the audience. She danced with him. Made a few cracks. And the curtain was brought down with a rush.'

Hundreds of viewers who had been watching the live broadcast from the theatre telephoned the television company and newspaper offices, demanding to know whether Pearl Bailey was drunk. But the drama that had been witnessed in millions of homes was nothing to the traumas that had been going on behind the scenes. Pearl Bailey, the preacher's daughter turned jazz singer, failed to turn up at the afternoon rehearsal. An hour before the show she was still asleep in her hotel bedroom.

Val Parnell told the show's compère, Tommy Trinder, to prepare an extra eight minutes 'just in case Miss Bailey doesn't make it'. Trinder walked on stage and, to his amazement, lolling in an armchair on one of the sets was Pearl Bailey. He reacted as if it was the most natural place on earth to discover the star of that night's show. 'Good evening, Miss Bailey,' he said politely. 'I'm the master of ceremonies.'

The reply was slurred and sardonic. 'Yes? What we have to put up with!'

Trinder spotted production assistant Charles Henry. 'She's drunk,' Trinder exclaimed. 'That's the understatement of the year,' replied Henry. 'She's paralytic. But Val wants her on. If she falls over you'd better go out and crack a few gags.'

Pearl Bailey's opening number, 'I'm Tired — Tired of the Blues,' went smoothly enough. Then came the sort of un-scheduled happening producers of live television shows have nightmares about. She climbed over the orchestra pit, landed in the front row of the stalls and strolled about, chatting to the audience.

In the television control van parked outside the theatre, the producer stared in disbelief at his deck of monitors. Behind the cameras, cues were discarded as cameramen fought to keep their lenses focused on the wandering star. At the side of the stage Henry tugged away at the microphone lead being trailed by the singer in an attempt to drag her back on stage.

At the end of the drama, Pearl Bailey sat in her dressing-room loquaciously reliving the nightmare performance. 'She's like a gramophone needle,' said her manager, Chauncey Olman. 'In all the fifteen years I've known her, I've never heard her go on talking for so long.'

Said Miss Bailey, 'All right, so it wasn't a good show. But believe me, the last thing I wanted to do was to go on that stage. I looked at those people down there and I felt that only they could help me. So down I went among them.' Was she drunk? 'I swear to you that I never had anything more than champagne in my life,' she said. 'And today I've not had one drop of that. I'm allergic to whisky and, for that matter, any other kind of spirits.'

Her doctors explained that she had been taking a combination of sodium amytal and a cortisone compound for nervousness and for an old injury to her left knee, and that these drugs could sometimes induce a feeling of elation and euphoria in the patient. The next day Pearl Bailey was visited by the then physician to the Queen, Dr. Ronald Bodley Scott. Her husband, jazz drummer Louis Belsen, announced: 'Pearl is a very, very sick woman. We are going home tomorrow.'

The following Sunday Tommy Trinder stepped on stage to the usual burst of applause. 'No, no, please,' he said, wickedly. 'I've got a shocking headache. I wanted to take some asprin. But after what happened here last week, I daren't.'

The booking of the legendary cabaret star Josephine Baker at the Palladium in 1974 was unscheduled and unheralded. Managing director Louis Benjamin was desperate, finding himself with a vacant week to fill in the middle of the August holidays after a cancellation by the scheduled star.

The deal was clinched and made public less than a fortnight before Miss Baker was to open. With so little time to sell to the theatre-going public a sixty-eight year old artist whom most had either forgotten or never heard of, it was hardly surprising that there was no mad rush for tickets. In 1925, there would have been a much more enthusiastic reaction. Miss Baker was then causing a sensation in a Paris show called 'La Revue Negre' in which she wore only a G-string of bananas. Nicknamed 'The Black Venus', she appeared regularly at the Casino de Paris and the Folies Begère.

The immensity of Josephine Baker's Palladium triumph can only be measured against the background of her truly amazing life. She was born in Missouri, USA of an African mother — her family being slaves from Sudan — and a Jewish father. At eight, young Josephine was singing in the clubs of Harlem. At fourteen, she was married. At eighteen, sickened by the racial intolerance of the American south, she packed her bags and sailed for Paris, where she discovered an affinity with a fascinating group of rootless young artists that included Hemingway, Matisse and Picasso. 'I used to look after them, pick up their clothes, get them organised. I was always popular because I was earning.'

At the outbreak of war 'The Black Venus' became 'The Singing Spy', when Captain Jacques Abtey enlisted her services for the military counter-espionage department. Her career as an entertainer was the perfect cover for the spying missions the captain had in mind, providing, as it did, the greatest possible freedom of movement for his agent. Together Jacques and Josephine embarked on missions that took them through Spain, Portugal, North Africa and the Middle East. For a time she was even attached to British Intelligence. Josephine Baker's heroic war efforts earned her the Chevalier Legion d'Honneur, Le Croix de Guerre and the Rosette de la Résistance.

She bought a fifteenth-century château in South-West France, ostensibly to raise cattle. Instead she raised children — twelve of them, from every corner of the globe, from Korea to Finland, from the Ivory Coast to Venezuela. The experiment was a costly one. In 1964 her château had amassed debts of £150,000. Brigitte Bardot made a television appeal for cash to help Josephine keep the adopted childred together. Five years later the battle was lost. Miss Baker was evicted by the police and forced to send her family to Paris.

It was against this background that The Black Venus arrived in London in 1974 to play the London Palladium for the first time.

Anyone in that first night audience who expected to see a matronly figure appear from the wings was in for a shock. She emerged wearing an ice blue cat-suit split to the navel, and a headdress of towering feathers, silk and jewels. Her legs were as shapely as an eighteen-year-old's. However, spotting a lady staring at her through a pair of theatre binoculars, she pleaded, 'Please don't do that — not for my sake, for your own. Don't shatter your illusions.'

She sang 'J'ai Deux Amours', the song with which she will forever be associated. She sang in English 'Along Came Bill'. She delivered a kaleidoscopic monologue that relived moving moments, recalled cherished companions, and went off to the rarest of accolades as a row of hardened theatre critics rose to their feet and cheered.

Such was Josephine Baker's impact during her eleven performances at the Palladium that she was invited back to London for the Royal Variety Performance. Of all the theatrical honours she had received during her life, this was her outstanding achievement. Six months afterwards, Josephine Baker, a truly great artist, was dead.

While Miss Baker was almost certainly the oldest leading lady at the Palladium, the record for being the youngest was held for quite some time by a girl from North London called Helen Shapiro. She was a fifteen-year-old schoolgirl with a throaty voice that belted out 'Walking Back to Happiness' when she first appeared at the theatre. However, Lena Zavaroni took the record from her on 16 March 1975 when she brought her precocious song and dance act to the stage at the tender age of eleven. While 2,300 people watched her live at the Palladium, millions more were sitting at home viewing a television show she had recorded some weeks earlier.

The little lass from Scotland rose to fame overnight via Hughie Green's television talent show, 'Opportunity Knocks'. By the time she was booked for the Palladium, Lena had appeared in America, met Frank Sinatra and Barbra Streisand

and been asked to sing for President Ford. If she was nervous on her Palladium début, she certainly did not show it. On two Sundays she strolled through four shows with the panache and confidence of a veteran performer – and then walked off stage to be transformed into a charming little girl again.

Palladium leading ladies have known their nights of disappointment, too. For the first ever Palladium bill on Boxing Day, 1910, American singer Ella Shields had prepared an entirely new act. She had chosen this historic night to launch herself on a new career as a male impersonator. So many acts were crowded into the show, that it was 11.45 before Ella went on. 'Sorry,' she was told, 'there's only time for you to sing one number now.' So Burlington Bertie had to wait to make his appearance another day.

A lady who would have considerable difficulty passing herself off as anything but female is the voluptuous Sabrina, whose vital statistics measure 42-18-35. Arthur Askey, who first presented her on television, said: 'When I danced with Sabrina, not only couldn't I see where I was going, I couldn't hear anything, either!' The decorative blonde was a surprise choice for the 1956 Royal Variety Performance. Unfortunately the show had to be cancelled at the eleventh hour because of the Suez crisis. Like many of her fellow artists, Sabrina was in tears. The following year when most of the invitations went to the stars of the previous show who had suffered such disappointment, Sabrina's name was not amongst them.

Sabrina left Britain to live in the States. Before returning in 1963, she wrote to Arthur Askey saying she would like her first appearance back in this country to be on his show since he had given her a start in show business. Askey had signed for a television show from the Palladium. When he received Sabrina's message he postponed his appearance so that she could join him in the show.

Another blonde, Betty Hutton – of the powerful voice – complained on her return to the Palladium that there were no hand microphones. 'What's happened to them?' she asked. 'You broke 'em all,' said producer Charlie Henry. He wasn't joking. Betty's frantic cavortings on stage during a previous

86

visit had cost the Palladium £1,000 in smashed microphones.

It was not the microphones but the dressing-room that Colette Gleeson, Tommy Steele's co-star in 'Hans Andersen', complained of. Like many of the older theatres, backstage at the Palladium is more functional than fashionable. Colette was so taken aback by her 'dungeon-like' room that she burst into tears and suggested to the management that she change into her costumes at home and travel to the theatre by taxi. 'At least,' she pleaded, 'put up some curtains, dab a spot of paint on the walls and fix a decent light. And please, please, could I possibly have a dressing table?' The management complied. Now the dressing-room has a chandelier, colour television, refrigerator and a carpet.

Cilla Black was equally dismayed by her room when she first starred at the theatre. She was at a loss to understand how the biggest names in show business had survived for so many years without a shower in the star dressing-room. She complained — and a shower room was installed.

Naturally a great theatre like the Palladium must have provided the background for a good many romances. Lynette Rae, for instance, was starring at the theatre when she met husband-to-be, Val Doonican, then a relatively unknown singer. Frank Windsor, who plays John Watt in television's 'Softly, Softly', used to wait most nights at the stage-door for dancer Mary Corbett. Now they are married. And Jack Douglas met his wife Susan when they were appearing together in the pantomime 'Cinderella', starring Max Bygraves and Julie Andrews — although it was hardly romance at first sight. Susan was just twelve years old when she made that Palladium appearance. Ten years later they met again, and fell in love.

The saddest leading lady of all must be Rumanian-born singer Magdalena Buznea. In October 1973 she hired the Palladium for a concert to commemorate the tenth anniversary of the death of Edith Piaf. Madame Buznea spent a £1,000 legacy from her late husband to finance the venture. Dorothy Squires sent her a good luck telegram.

The concert set a new record for the Palladium. Only two hundred people bought tickets for the show.

Beat the Clock

FEATHER OF BIRDS A TOGETHER STICK
'Right, my love, don't be nervous. All you have to do is
arrange the words on the board into a well-known phrase
or saying. You have thirty seconds to Beat the Clock . . .
starting from now!'
BIRDS OF A FEATHER STICK TOGETHER
'You've done it! Well done, my love. Angela, open the
curtains.' (Oooooh! from the audience) 'Marvellous!
You have won tonight's star prize — a magnificent
eighteen-inch television with press button controls and
all three channels!'

It was 8 pm on 25 September 1955 when Val Parnell's 'Sunday
Night at the London Palladium' first appeared on the TV screen
— with more of a whimper than a bang. Gracie Fields and
Guy Mitchell were topping the bill, but only 387,000 viewers
saw the show, an audience rating that would hardly do
justice to the 'Epilogue' today. But Independent Television
was in its infancy — three days old to be exact, and available
only to viewers in the London area. And the majority of those
possessed BBC-only receivers.

Parnell was now playing a dual role, as boss of Moss
Empires and managing director of Associated Television — at
that time the London Weekend station. But his first love was

88

(ATV) (News of the World)

The Crazy Gang

Morecambe and Wise, 1963

It's 'Beat the Clock' time with Bruce Forsyth on 'Sunday Night at the London Palladium

*Don
Arrol*

*Norman
Vaughan*

(ATV)

Jim Dale

Ted Rogers

Jimmy
Tarbuck

Bob
Monkhouse

Jimmy Jewel and Ben Warriss

*Stan Laurel and Oliver Hardy with Dolores Gray at the Royal Variety Show,
1947*

(Keystone

the theatre, and one theatre in particular – the London Palladium. 'Sunday Night at the London Palladium' was Parnell's baby. He conceived it, delivered it, nurtured it, cherished it, corrected it when it went astray until, while still only a precocious child of five, it was mature enough to determine the Sunday evening viewing habits of almost half the nation. A vicar in Woking was quick to recognise the fact, and brought the time of his Sunday Evensong forward half-an-hour so that the congregation could get home to see the show. 'It's no use hiding the fact that "Sunday Night at the Palladium" is more popular than going to church on a cold winter's night,' he said resignedly.

In January 1960 Cliff Richard sang to nineteen and a half million viewers. In February Max Bygraves drew twenty-one million, and in December the same year Harry Secombe captured an audience of twenty-two million, a record that was never broken – quite an achievement when you consider some of the great entertainers who followed Harry Secombe on the Palladium magic roundabout: Sammy Davis Jr., Danny Kaye (again), Bob Hope, Judy Garland, Ella Fitzgerald, Jane Russell, Howard Keel, Johnnie Ray, Sophie Tucker, Liberace, Mario Lanza, Nat King Cole, Pat Boone, Eartha Kitt and Connie Francis, as well as the biggest names in British Variety.

Parnell's philosophy was simple: 'I'm offering television viewers a seat in the circle at the greatest Variety theatre in the world to watch the finest artists money can buy.' The Palladium show had to be something more than just another TV programme. Parnell wanted viewers to feel they had really put on their finery and gone out for a night at the theatre; as he once explained, 'That is why the cameras always show the full sweep of the Palladium as the curtain goes up, focusing on the audience as well as the stage.' In the early shows the illusion was carried a stage further – the opening sequence showed a pretty girl in the stalls slowly turning the pages of a theatre programme.

Three distinct features characterised 'Sunday Night at the London Palladium': the star name at the top of the bill; 'Beat the Clock'; and the comedians who compèred the show.

93

More than twenty artists have introduced 'Sunday Night at the London Palladium' — a fact which, in itself, is surprising. When most people think back to the Palladium and its compères, only four names spring readily to mind, three of which became household names and four-figure-a-week stars after their sojourn at the Palladium. The fourth was a big star of a previous decade who was making a comeback to the British show business scene. Their style of comedy could hardly have been more of a contrast, their line of patter more diverse. What they had in common was good material, a rapport with their audience, a grass-roots appeal — and an instantly recognisable catchphrase. Their names are Bruce ('I'm in charge') Forsyth; Norman ('swinging — dodgy') Vaughan; Jimmy ('Boom, Boom') Tarbuck and old peninsular chin himself, Tommy ('You lucky people') Trinder.

Trinder's run as a regular Palladium bill topper, which had begun with 'Band Waggon' in 1939, came to an end in 1950 when he starred in the pantomime 'Puss in Boots' and an autumn show called 'Starlight Rendezvous'. The Palladium had by then become the domain of American entertainers, and Trinder went off to the Antipodes in search of a new audience. The Australians found this egocentric Pommie's coarse cockney humour akin to their own, and soon Trinder was earning £1,500 a week. He bought a block of flats in Sydney and discovered a profitable additional source of income making commercials for sausages. He had intended to stay there for only six months, but it was more than two years before he returned to Britain and 'Cinderella on Ice' at London's Empress Hall. A few months later he was skating on thinner ice when he accepted Parnell's invitation to compère his new Palladium television show. While Trinder had been away, a new batch of comics had sprung to the fore through their appearances on the small screen, amongst them Benny Hill, Tony Hancock and Norman Wisdom. Now Trinder had the chance to compete with the newcomers on their own ground. He was booked for six Palladium shows. 'After those six weeks nobody said "Don't come any more", so I kept going.' Trinder says.

94

The show grew from its London-based audience to the national Independent Television network. 'I never got any more money. Mind, I didn't ask for it. To me, the Palladium show was a bit of fun. It wasn't real television. It was what I had always known — standing up in a theatre in front of an audience.'

Trinder started the tradition of topical jokes, setting a pattern his successors were happy to follow. He spent every Sunday morning scanning the newspapers for possible material. People in the news were always good for a laugh. Only occasionally did the 'victims' object. 'One person I had to be careful with was Liberace,' remembers Trinder. 'It wasn't he who got upset, but his temperamental fans. One night I said, "The Army made a man out of Liberace — and he sued them". The next morning you couldn't see my desk for letters of protest.'

Trinder's experience as a stand-up comic stood him in good stead the night the power line to the theatre failed and the show could not be transmitted at the scheduled time. The producer was anxious to keep the audience in their seats until the show could be broadcast — in those days transmissions were live — and suggested to Trinder that he go on stage and entertain them. Trinder obliged — for one-and-a-half hours. When the power was finally restored, the producer came on stage and said, 'Ladies and gentlemen, thank you very much for being so patient.' As Trinder walked off he quipped, 'Ladies and gentlemen, you have just witnessed an example of man's ingratitude to man.' It was around 10 pm before the show went on the air. 'Welcome to Monday morning at the London Palladium,' said Tommy, greeting the viewers.

Trinder's six-week engagement stretched from September 1955 to June 1957. His dismissal was abrupt; in fact he knew nothing of it until he read a sentence in the show business newspaper, *The Stage*, which stated quite simply that Dickie Henderson was joining the Palladium TV show. 'Nobody ever said a word to me. Nobody said goodbye,' says Trinder ruefully. It was ironic, as not long before the television company had presented the comedian with a solid gold cigarette box.

The inscription read, 'To Tommy Trinder, who has abundantly proved on many occasions to be ATV's Man of the Year — 1956, Val Parnell.'

Dickie Henderson was followed by Bob Monkhouse, Hughie Green, Alfred Marks and even actor Robert Morley. Topical gags were written on cue cards and held up in the orchestra pit for the compère to read. 'Trouble was, the boys didn't always hold up the cards in the right order,' Alfred Marks remembers.

It was 11 September 1958 when Bruce Forsyth took over. On his opening show he plunged straight in. 'I suppose you lot are wondering how I got this job? Well, I went to the Labour Exchange and the fellow there took one look at me and said, "Yes, I've got a job for you. I hear Val Parnell is looking for a new face. Well, your clock would take some beating, wouldn't it?" I said, "Looking for a new face is he? So am I, mate. I'm sick of the sight of this one!" '

Getting a laugh at his own expense immediately endeared Forsyth to his audience. 'Once that joke got a laugh, I was away,' he says. 'I made up my mind to be a different sort of compère. The public had thought of a compère as someone who came on and told a couple of jokes between acts. I decided to try to work out individual routines; if my first appearance was a success and I was asked back, I would build up bits with a piano, try out double acts with other performers on the bill.'

That was the way it worked out. Forsyth's versatility — he started in the business as a song-and-dance-man, switching to comedy only four years before — his exuberance and self-confidence, quickly established him as a firm favourite with viewers.

Trinder's catchphrase 'You lucky people!' had been around almost as long as the comic himself. Forsyth's came about by accident. A jolly lady named Beattie came on the show as a contestant in 'Beat the Clock'. All the time she was on stage she argued good-naturedly with Bruce, ignoring his instructions on how the games should be played and insisting on organising the whole charade her way. Suddenly Bruce shouted at the top of his voice, 'Listen, Beattie, I'm in charge here.'

The remark brought a laugh, but nobody imagined it had made a lasting impression. A few days later the ATV studio manager Jim Smith overheard two technicians talking, when one of them turned to the other and said, 'Listen, I'm in charge!' Smith stood there trying to remember where he had heard the phrase before. 'Then it hit me,' he says. 'I took Bruce aside and told him he should try to work the line in again the following week.'

Forsyth did. And soon the whole nation was saying 'I'm in charge.' He was so grateful to the lady who started it all that he invited her back on the show as his special guest.

Forsyth could hold his own with any of the big-name stars he introduced. But one gag did backfire on him. Robert Horton, who had made a tremendous impact on television audiences as the star of the Western series, 'Wagon Train', was flown to London to appear in the Palladium show. The scene outside the theatre was reminiscent of the hysteria which had greeted Sinatra, Johnnie Ray and Danny Kaye a few years before. Inside, the Palladium curtains opened to reveal a tall man with his back to the audience, dressed in buckskin jacket and Wild West stetson. Girls shrieked and tore at their hair. Slowly the figure turned round. And – 'Caught you there,' said Forsyth. Horton's fans could not see the joke – and they let Bruce know in no uncertain fashion.

Forsyth was plucked out of a summer show in Eastbourne to make his Palladium début. He was initially engaged for just one night. He stayed for two years – it was the longest one-night stand on record.

Forsyth's successor was a baby-faced, nervous-looking comedian named Don Arrol, and though the hearts of the viewing mums went out to him, his reign was short-lived, and in 1961 Forsyth came back. But the strain of doing weekday Variety, cabaret appearances and 'Sunday Night at the London Palladium' – he was at the theatre by 11 am and never left much before 10 pm – proved too much. Forsyth suffered a nervous breakdown and his doctor ordered him to rest.

Thus in January 1962, another unknown seized his big

chance. Within a few months everything was 'swinging' for Liverpool-born Norman Vaughan. His catchphrases — 'swinging', accompanied by a thumbs-up sign, and 'dodgy' accompanied by a thumbs-down — were echoed all over the country in reaction to good or bad news. The Labour Party even seriously considered using the slogan for an election campaign — 'Swinging with Labour; Dodgy with the Tories'. Eventually they plumped for 'Let's go with Labour', but the posters still bore a huge upturned thumb. They weren't the only catchphrases Vaughan used; there was also 'a touch of the. . .' and 'it's all happening', which have since become common parlance and are used all the time by disc jockeys.

'I had a running gag based on the events of television's "Coronation Street",' recalls Vaughan. 'Each week I would crack a joke about one of the characters or an incident in that week's episodes. The gag that got me the biggest laugh came during the drama over Dennis Tanner being suspected by the police of stealing some money. I walked on stage very slowly and said *sotto voce*, "Dennis Tanner — he didn't take that money, you know." It brought the house down.' Wherever Norman Vaughan appeared, the audience shouted for jokes about 'Coronation Street'. At an American airforce base he was greeted with the shout, 'How's Ena?'

During the John Profumo affair, Vaughan was warned that any gags about Christine Keeler, Mandy Rice Davies or other personalities involved in the pending court case, were sub judice. He and scriptwriter Eric Merriman racked their brains for a way round the ban. As it turned out, it was what he did not say on stage that brought the laugh. He told the audience, 'It's all been happening this week — but I can't say a word about it.'

Off-stage Vaughan bristles with nervous energy. Yet he seemed calm enough on that important first Sunday in the compère's spot. Parnell invited him and the star of the show, Tommy Steele, to lunch. The new compère tucked enthusiastically into his food. 'Gawd,' said Steele. 'How on earth can you eat like that on a day like this?' It might have been the reaction of a condemned man presented with his last meal, for Vaughan always suffered agonies before a show. 'Nothing in show business can match the ordeal of a live television performance,' he says. 'I never slept a wink the night before the show. I would get abdominal migraine. It would start in my head and drop into my stomach until I vomited. Often I was in agony only minutes before the curtain went up.'

Parnell was taking no chances with his newest discovery. After Forsyth's breakdown, he was determined it should not happen again, and when the Palladium show was off the air for one week, he packed Vaughan off to a London clinic. Nobody ever knew, and he was back compèring the show the following Sunday.

The Forsyth saga resumed at the Palladium in September 1963. Thereafter he and Norman Vaughan took it in turns to compère the show.

Eric Merriman would telephone Vaughan each Saturday after 'Match of the Day' with suggestions for the topical gags. Often they would still be discussing the routine in the early hours of Sunday morning — and the whole script might need revamping in the build-up to the actual performance. In May 1965 Vaughan decided that enough was enough. The Palladium show was going through something of a crisis and steadily slipping down the ratings chart. At the beginning of 1965 it was number one in the popularity stakes; by May it had slumped to nineteenth position. Some of the regional television companies threatened to drop the programme unless it was given a new look.

The 'new look' came in the shape of a Beatle-haired extrovert from Liverpool named Jimmy Tarbuck. He had all the cockiness and brashness of Trinder, plus the kind of appeal that would draw a much-needed younger audience. Tarbuck had grown up in the shadow of the Beatles. He had learned his trade touring the country with the crop of pop singers who had climbed onto the Merseyside bandwagon. 'Of course, the kids hadn't come to see a comic,' says Tarbuck. 'They were there to have a good scream at their dream idols. They never listened to me.' At one concert someone even threw an ice-cream at him. He licked it and managed to quip, 'Ah vanilla. The flavour of the month.' But 'Sunday Night at the London Palladium' turned him into a sex symbol overnight. He would leave the theatre to find his car daubed with loving messages written in lipstick. He was mobbed wherever he went. He admitted he could not dance like Forsyth or Vaughan, and he was not the greatest singer in the world. But he was fortunate enough to be around at the time of the Liverpool craze, and he seized his opportunity eagerly.

One Sunday a 'Three Musketeers' sketch was included in the show. Tarbuck changed into his d'Artagnan costume only to be told that the show was over-running and the sketch would have to be cut. There was no time to change back into a suit. He had to walk on, crack a joke and introduce the next artist, inexplicably dressed as a musketeer. Mystified, Tarbuck's mother telephoned her son. 'You were very good,' she said. 'But what on earth possessed you to wear that fancy dress?'

In 1966 the first Anglo-American version of the show was produced. The Palladium show was seen in colour for the first time – but only in the United States. In Britain, Independent Television was still limited to black and white. Compères for the joint series were chosen for their appeal on both sides of the Atlantic. Lorne Greene, star of the TV Western series 'Bonanza' hosted the first show, followed by Hugh O'Brian, Fess Parker, Kate Smith, Jonathan Winters and Roger Moore.

In 1967 'Sunday Night at the London Palladium' came to an end as a regular series. Bob Monkhouse compèred the final show which starred Forsyth, Vaughan and Tarbuck.

One other comic hosted the show – the late Arthur Haynes. And he knew nothing about it until he stepped off a train at Euston a few hours before the programme. The Palladium had been thrown into panic that morning when the regular compère fell ill. Someone remembered that Arthur Haynes was appearing in Birmingham and could quickly be transported to London. By the time the comedian was tracked down, he was already heading towards the capital. He received the surprise of his life when his train pulled in and an

ATV welcoming committee was there to greet him. He might have expected to see Eamonn Andrews step out and announce, 'This is your life.' Instead, he was asked 'Will you compère tonight's Palladium show?'

He had not only to memorise the gags, but also to learn the games in record time. For, until Tarbuck's tenure of office, part of every compère's role was to utter the magic words *'It's Beat the Clock Time!'*

'Beat the Clock' was a product of American television. Parnell saw it, liked the idea of audience participation that it involved, and clinched a deal to sandwich 'Beat the Clock' between the show's two commercial breaks.

The concept was simple. Basically 'Beat the Clock' was a series of party games played by members of the audience on stage. They consisted of throwing balls at targets, balancing cups and saucers, keeping balloons in the air while clambering into baggy trousers or Wellington boots, or negotiating blindfold a simple obstacle course. One game required two blindfold contestants to locate each other and kiss within sixty seconds, making only kissing sounds to guide them towards each other.

The early shows relied on games borrowed from the American show, and it was an unsuspecting summer show audience at the Windmill Theatre in Great Yarmouth who acted as guinea pigs when they were first tried out in this country. Palladium show producer Albert Locke took a carload of props and £100 in cash to Yarmouth where Tommy Trinder was appearing. With the theatre management's permission, Trinder stopped the show and introduced the audience to the joys of 'Beat the Clock'. 'We had agreed to do twenty minutes,' says Locke. 'But Tommy was loving it, dashing about the stage handing out fivers. It was forty-five minutes before we called a halt.'

More important, the audience liked 'Beat the Clock', too. There were a lot of rough edges to smooth, but the games played that week in Great Yarmouth provided the nucleus of the party fare during the first tentative weeks of the Palladium television show.

Contestants were chosen each Sunday during the compère's warm-up session with his audience. Usually they were married couples. Honeymooners were always a popular choice, and provided the compère with a few easy laughs: 'How long have you been married, my luv? Two days! So you're on your honeymoon?' — feigning astonishment — 'What on earth are you doing up at this time?'

Each compère had his own line of patter for selecting the contestants, but the formula hardly changed. 'Anyone from Wigan?. . . Is there a doctor in the house — with his wife?. . . I'd like a couple from the stalls, another from the dress circle, and a pair from the gods. I don't want anybody who is elderly or has a disability. Nor do I want a lady who is expecting anything other than a prize.' The audience roars with laughter. But the qualifications are serious. The 'Sunday Night at the London Palladium' crew still have nightmares about the contestant who presented 'Beat the Clock' with its most embarrassing moment. Everything was running smoothly until Tommy Trinder introduced the final game. It was simple enough. All the contestant had to do was knock a balloon into the air, run across the stage, build a small wall of bricks, dash back before the balloon fell to the ground, knock it back up, run back, build some more of the wall . . . and so on. The object of the game was to complete the wall in an allotted time.

The man said he understood the rules and Trinder gave the 'off'. The fellow knocked the balloon into the air all right, but seemed to have difficulty in running. Suddenly the truth dawned on Trinder — the contestant had a club-foot. He reacted quickly to prevent any further embarrassment, grabbing the brick and completing the game himself. Angry viewers telephoned ATV and the Palladium to complain. And thereafter it was made a rule always to check a contestant's feet first.

Trinder was involved in another embarrassing incident — but this time it was calculated to make the contestants blush.

A husband and wife successfully completed the games and went home with a magnificent canteen of cutlery. Trinder, in his enthusiasm for the prize, was perhaps guilty of slightly over-selling it. 'There you are,' he told the couple, 'a wonderful canteen of cutlery worth at least £200.' Within days a solicitor's letter arrived at the ATV offices. The winners had sent the prize to be valued and discovered it was worth only £80. Would the Palladium kindly forward the balance of £120 forthwith?

Trinder was furious. On the following week's programme he pulled the letter from his pocket and read it out verbatim. Not another word was heard from the couple, or their solicitor.

'Beat the Clock' was never short of critics. Newspaper reviewers called it 'degrading' and 'an insult to human dignity'. But in fact, Jim Smith — the man who dreamed up the games — and Albert Locke went out of their way to ensure that contestants were not made to look ridiculous. Slapstick games with the players getting doused with water and goo, and lots of custard-pie throwing — popular in the States — were outlawed.

Many of Smith's ideas were gleaned from wandering around toyshops looking at the latest novelties. He became an avid reader of toy catalogues. Monday was set aside as games day, when he would sit rooted to his desk with a pencil and a blank sheet of paper until inspiration came. Not until Friday on the Palladium stage would he discover whether his ideas actually proved feasible, when stage hand Fred Pearson and electrician Norman Stone tested them out.

The jackpot was the climax of 'Beat the Clock'. At a certain point in every session, a bell would ring to signal that the couple involved in games at that moment were the contestants lucky enough to get a crack at the jackpot game, which was always far more difficult. Prize money began at £100. Each week that the prize was not won, the money increased by a further £100, and the jackpot game remained unchanged until a couple were successful.

The largest sum ever won on the Palladium show was £1,300. It went to a sailor and his wife who lived in Birmingham; to earn it the wife had to bounce tennis balls to her husband on the opposite side of the stage, while he caught them in sequence in boxes perched on the end of a pole. After this, ITA limited the prize money to £1,000.

People often wondered whether it was actually possible to win a jackpot game. They did not know that every game had to pass the Norman-Fred test before being included on the show, and even then, they were always made a little easier for the actual contestants, who would naturally be under considerable strain. Even so, for eighteen weeks one game defied every couple who attempted it. It consisted of bouncing a ball off a bass drum onto a snare drum and a cymbal, before being caught by the lady contestant. Week by week the prize money mounted. Week by week more and more viewers sat glued to their sets willing the contestants to win the jackpot. But the game eluded them all, and eventually it was taken off and the £1,800 that had accumulated shared amongst four charities. Yet when the game was resurrected for a charity show at the Festival Hall, thirteen couples completed it with no trouble at all. Later, it was brought back for 'Sunday Night at the London Palladium', and this time the money was won in the second week.

One contestant managed to beat the clock, but was less successful at beating the law. The fellow volunteered to enter with a woman he introduced as his wife. The couple won their games, collected their prizes and left. Next morning Jim Smith received a telephone call, purportedly from Scotland Yard. The caller was inquiring about the name and address of one of the previous night's contestants. Smith explained that he was reluctant to release that sort of information in case it exposed the contestants to begging letters and visits from cranks. He would have to ring back to check that the call really was from Scotland Yard. Sure enough, when he dialled the Whitehall number, the caller turned out to be a high-ranking officer at the Yard, who explained that the fellow on the Palladium show had been on the Liverpool police files for a number of years. He was wanted on a serious charge and was on the run. The inspector in charge of the case was a Palladium devotee and had spotted the wanted man on the previous night's show. After his exposure on the Palladium stage, the criminal was soon arrested.

He was not the only winner to end up a loser. An Inland Revenue inspector spotted a 'client' who had done a disappearing act some time before. The fellow was duly traced and nabbed for back taxes.

It was not just the critics who objected to 'Beat the Clock': in 1961 a Yorkshireman devised a novel means of stopping the clock. Each week, at exactly the time 'Beat the Clock' was broadcast, the saboteur would snip through the television cable relaying the programme to four hundred homes. However, whatever the critics and the occasional lunatic thought, the mass of the Sunday viewing public loved the show. Whenever it was publicly suggested that 'Beat the Clock' be dropped, there was an outcry, and on one particular night a deputation turned up at the Palladium and threatened to start a riot unless they were given a categorical assurance that it would not be axed. In fact, 'Beat the Clock' survived ten years as a regular buffer spot on 'Sunday Night at the London Palladium.' If the show over-ran, this could be rectified by trimming back on the games. But whichever game was dropped, 'Beat the Clock' always ended with the 'Word Game' — the wife or girlfriend being asked to sort out a jumble of words on a magnetic board into a well-known phrase or saying.

Prizes were usually television sets, record players, washing machines or cookers, and there was always an attractive young hostess to hand the gifts over. One girl, blonde Angela Bracewell, appeared on the show for six years, had a pop song, 'Angela', dedicated to her, and was pursued at the stage door for months by an American multi-millionaire. 'He's a pain in the neck,' said Angela, and politely returned his flowers and expensive gifts.

By the 326th show, a mathematical genius calculated that Jim Smith had devised 1,498 games, 749 contestants had participated, and £16,300 had been won in prizes.

When Tarbuck took over as compère 'Beat the Clock' was dropped. It was brought back, however, in 1973 — a year after Parnell's death — when ATV boss Sir Lew Grade restored the Palladium show to the Sunday night screens.

To viewers with long memories it seemed nothing had changed. Back came the Tiller Girls; back came the familiar 'Starlight' theme composed by Eric Rogers that had introduced every Palladium show; back came the compère, only now it was an all-rounder called Jim Dale; and back came the revolving stage on which the artists appearing in the show always waved goodbye. The 'Beat the Clock' that came back, however, wore a new look and had a new name: 'Anything You Can Do'. This time all the prize money went to charity; but even if the whole thing was more streamlined and whisked along at a faster pace, underneath it was still the same old 'Beat the Clock'. The donation of the prize money to charity was a noble gesture, even though it begged the question: should the gift of a guide dog for the blind depend upon the deftness of a man with a spiked helmet on his head bursting a stageful of balloons in a given time?

The programme failed to re-establish itself in the TV ratings; twice a bomb hoax call cleared the theatre and kept the top of the bill off the screen, and the cost of each show had escalated to £50,000 — compared with £8,000 in 1955 and £20,000 in 1965. By the fourth month desperate ATV executives were calling out the lifeboats to save their sinking Ocean Queen. Albert Locke came out of retirement to take charge of production; the exuberant Second Generation team of dancers replaced the Tiller Girls; and Ted Rogers took over from Jim Dale as compère. Rogers won rave notices, but the show flopped. It ended its run in the spring, and has never returned.

There was a light-hearted moment on one of the bomb hoax occasions. When the all-clear was given the artists returned to finish the show. At the finale, one star was missing. 'Where's Charlie?' everyone asked. Then, as the stage began to revolve, a sinister figure appeared out of the darkness of the wings,

raincoat collar turned up, hat pulled low over the eyes —
carrying a 'bomb'. The fuse was well alight, and for a second
people held their breath. 'Hello, my darlin's,' said the figure.
It was Charlie Drake, and the bomb was courtesy of the prop
room.

'Sunday Night at the London Palladium', which had come
in with a whimper nineteen years before, had so very nearly
gone out with a bang.

Bring on the Dancing Girls

The dancing troupe most closely associated with the London Palladium is the Tiller Girls. The girls look alike, they dress alike, and because of their precise, regimented dance routines, if you stand at the end of the line you will see twenty pairs of arms and twenty pairs of legs moving as one.

The choreographical inspiration came from the guardsmen on the parade square. John Tiller, who founded the troupe in the late 1800s, marvelled at their clockwork timing, comparing it with the ragged movements of the chorus lines in the majority of stage productions he watched. Tiller ran a thriving business and held a seat on the Lancashire Cotton Exchange. For amusement he dabbled in the production side of amateur theatricals. When he was still in his thirties, he was ruined in the cotton crash and turned to the theatre to re-build his lost fortune.

He opened a dancing school, and in a room with bare boards he would rehearse his girls until they cried with pain. Often the older ones would be made to practise from nine in the morning until midnight. They would walk home in their stockings — their feet too sore and blistered to put into shoes.

The first Tiller troupe comprised just four girls. They were launched in 1886 as the Four Little Rosebuds and were an immediate success. Tiller trained more girls, and formed other troupes. From the beginning discipline was strict. A senior

Marie Lloyd

Gracie Fields and Gigli, 1952

The Tiller Girls, 1973 . . .

. . . and in 1906

(Sun)

. . . backstage

(Crown Copyright)

(Sun)

Lena Zavaroni

(inset): Palladium tradition: Rosemary
Clooney leaves a good luck message on
her dressing-room mirror for the room's
next occupant

Josephine Baker with Palladium housekeeper Rose Summers

(Su

girl was appointed captain of each troupe and it was her duty to see that her charges went straight from the theatre to their lodgings, avoided undesirable acquaintances and habits, kept themselves neat and clean, and had a weekly 'make and mend' session on their clothes. Tiller's wife Jenny presided over them all like a mistress at a girls' preparatory school. She even insisted on meeting and approving would-be husbands.

The Tiller Girls went from strength to strength. In 1912 a troupe appeared before King George V and Queen Mary in a royal Variety bill that included George Robey, Harry Lauder, Anna Pavlova, and Little Titch. A Tiller troupe was the original 'Les Girls' in the Folies Bergère in Paris, and Flo Ziegfeld booked them for his Follies on Broadway.

When Tiller died his schools of dancing — there were now several — were left in the care of three employees: Robert Smith and Doris Alloway, who looked after the administration, and Barbara Aitken, the choreographer — a role she still occupies today. She started as a Tiller girl herself, and was auditioned by the founder of the school. She remembers the Tillers' first appearance at the Palladium. After that particular show closed, with no apparent offer of a re-engagement, the girls accepted a booking in Berlin. When a message arrived asking them to appear at the Palladium, it was too late. A 'reserve' troupe had to be drafted in.

By the early 'fifties there were nine Tiller troupes appearing in pantomimes up and down the country, and well over two hundred girls on the dancing schools' books. Not even the meagre salary of £7 a week could deter the aspiring youngsters, or their mothers. They wrote in their hundreds begging to be given a chance on the boards.

Jane Clombies was one such girl. A willowy blonde, Jane was one of the few Tillers actually to make her first professional appearance with a troupe at the Palladium. She remembers those days as both glamorous and exciting — but sometimes embarrassing and perilous, too. Like the night during a guardsmen's routine when her busby slipped lower and lower over her face until she couldn't see at all. 'I've got to get off,' she shouted. 'You can't do that,' said the girl next to her in the line. 'Just carry on dancing and I'll shout out the directions.' Or the night the straps of her halter-neck dress snapped. Jane completed the routine with her arms crossed in front of her. The doubtful honour of being the first topless Tiller fell to another young lady. The night her straps snapped, she just let the dress slip down and danced on without a blush.

There was the night a Tiller Girl's frilly panties dropped to her ankles. Unabashed, she stepped out of them and carried on dancing, even though her high kicks were aimed a little lower that night. A dancer in the famous French Bluebell troupe suffered a similar kind of embarrassment during Ken Dodd's Palladium revue, 'Doddy's Here Again'. The girls were dancing on a staircase when a ball of rubber padding popped out of the dancer's brassière and bounced its way down the flight of stairs, much to the amusement of the audience. The padding rolled gently to the wings, and came to rest at the feet of a stage hand. As the girl came off, scarlet-faced, the young man returned the padding with a chirpy, 'Excuse me, miss. I think you lost something.'

Kay Lambert, captain of a Tiller troupe that appeared in the 1948 Royal Variety Performance, remembers the night the Tillers weren't quite in tune. 'It happened during a pantomime. Sixteen of us had to ring hand bells, each pair of girls being given a different note to play, so that together we rang a complete octave. This night our act was brought forward at the last minute and we had to make a mad dash from the dressing-room to the stage, grabbing the bells as we went. Unbeknown to us, someone had got them mixed up. As we were late there was no time for the usual check tinkle. I can still hear the ear-splitting din as we started to ring those bells!'

A chandelier routine provided another ear-shattering occasion. It was a glittering spectacle, with the girls' costumes bedecked with sparkling beads and sequins, and an imitation chandelier suspended over the stage. As the dancers reached the end of the routine they moved forward to take their bow. Suddenly there was a mighty crash, and the chandelier smashed down in the exact spot where the girls had been dancing only seconds before. So disciplined were the Tillers that not one girl looked round.

The guidelines for selecting a Tiller girl have remained essentially unchanged: height around 5 feet 4 inches, bust 34 inches, waist 24 inches, hips 35 inches. The girl has to be pleasant-looking, intelligent, have previous dancing experience, and, above all, be a 'refined young lady'.

Should a dancer put on a few surplus pounds, Barbara Aitken has a simple remedy. 'Nothing,' she insists, 'brings down your weight as quickly as skipping. It is more effective than any diet. A hundred skips a day is all you need.' She has put so many girls on her slimming course that 'a hundred skips a day' has become a stock joke amongst the Tillers.

For many years the girls learned the Tiller technique in an old chapel near Cambridge Circus, where John Wesley once preached. Hour after hour they practised in front of long mirrors. 'One, out, up, in, kick . . . one, out, up, in, kick.' Counting, ceaseless counting – that is the secret. When a step is mastered, two girls attempt it together, practising until their legs, arms, heads and bodies move as one. A third girl is added to the line, then a fourth – until sixteen or twenty dancers are moving with total precision, perfectly in step.

'Being Tillerised means smoothing out the individualists,' says Kay Lambert. 'In an ordinary chorus line, although she is doing the same step, every girl has her own particular style. Usually she is hoping to be noticed and picked out for a solo part.' Tiller's teaching was different. From the moment a Tiller steps on stage she has to lose her identity. A dancer does not try to kick for the highest point she can reach, but for one she knows everyone else in the troupe can attain.

One myth that can be exploded is the assumption that the girls are all of uniform height. The illusion is created by placing the tallest dancers at the end of the line and the shortest in the middle. So successfully did the trick work, that Wendy Clark at 5 feet 3½ inches was able to dance in the same line as Jane Clombies, who is 5 feet 7 inches. 'But it did mean we little ones had to kick higher,' says Wendy. 'I suppose we were pretty fit. You had to be. For some unaccountable reason the Tillers' dressing-room always seemed to be furthest away from the stage, up countless stairs. Crazy when you think that we usually had the most changes of costume. In one show we wore fourteen costumes. It was nothing to witness half-naked females dashing up the stairs shedding items of clothing as they went.'

Jane Clombies recalls a quick-change that did not go quite as planned. There was no time to reach the dressing-room, so the dancers had to swap costumes at the side of the stage. Everything was fine until Jane stepped into a pair of shoes that had been conveniently placed in the wings for her. 'I tried to walk back on stage and my feet wouldn't move. The shoes had been nailed to the floor . . . and a row of grinning faces were peering round the curtains.' It was a favourite jape of the Crazy Gang, and many of that night's audience must have spent the next few minutes wondering why fifteen dancers were in black shoes and only one in white.

Practical jokes are normally reserved for the last night. A favourite trick of the orchestra is to play faster and faster in the hope the girls will exhaust themselves trying to keep up with the music and collapse in a heap on stage. Another pastime of the boys in the pit is to draw diagrams of the girls' legs, plotting exactly where the holes in their tights are each night.

Robert Luff, the impresario who created the stage version of the 'Black and White Minstrel Show' which stars another famous dancing troupe, the Television Toppers, took over the running of the Tiller Girls in 1973. That year the Tillers enjoyed a brief resurgence when 'Sunday Night at the London Palladium' returned to the television screen. At the end of the series they went back to Bournemouth and Brighton.

Only two Tiller troupes now appear on a regular basis. The more liberated dancing of the Young Generation, the Second Generation and Pan's People is now the vogue. On Palladium Variety bills now it is Dougie Squires's Second Generation and not the Tillers who open the second half of the bill. But Robert Luff insists there will always be room for the dancing troupe a Lancashire cotton dealer founded nearly ninety years ago. 'They are a show business institution,' he says. 'In all my years in the game I have never known a troupe of dancers who could draw such a warm response from an audience as the Tillers.'

Watch Out! The Gang's In

The curtain had long since come down, the stalls had emptied and, in the dressing-rooms, the greasepaint had been packed away for another night. Cigar smoke made patterns in the still air as it drifted its way from a round table in the corner of the Palladium bar. A babble of voices could be heard, slurred voices, affected by several hours of steady drinking.

One voice was raised in anger. George Black, the master showman, was displeased, venting his wrath on a diminutive figure in the centre of the group. 'Just watch it, or you'll be out,' he rasped.

The little fellow downed his drink, shrugged his shoulders and slouched towards the door. Under his breath he mumbled, 'I don't care what G. B. says — he's £30,000 too late.'

Jimmy Gold could afford to be blasé. As a member of the Crazy Gang he was one of the highest-paid comics in the country — and thrifty enough to have put sufficient of that £30,000 aside for a rainy day. Once, when a fellow performer passed a billboard bearing the message 'The Lord Saves', he turned to his companion and quipped, 'I bet not as much as Jimmy Gold.'

That night at the Palladium, 'Monsewer' Eddie Gray put his arm round Gold's shoulders and said sympathetically, 'Come on, Jimmy, I'll drive you home.' In the car, Gold continued muttering and cursing. 'I don't give a damn what

George Black says,' he said. 'He's £25,000 too late.' Eddie Gray slammed on the brakes, tugged at the steering wheel, did a sharp U-turn round the Cenotaph and roared back along Whitehall.

Jimmy Gold was jerked back to sobriety. 'What's wrong?' he asked. 'Where are you going?'

'I'm heading back to the theatre, mate,' said Eddie. 'You've dropped £5,000 between here and the Palladium.'

The Crazy Gang were visual performers — words cannot do justice to their genius as slapstick comedians. Yet, to leave them out of a work on the London Palladium would be a grave omission.

They were in residence at the Palladium for eight triumphant — and at times, tumultuous — years, although it was not until their sixth year that they were collectively billed as 'The Crazy Gang'. George Black was apprehensive when the first revue in which they appeared opened on 30 November 1931. Nothing could have been further from his mind than a long tenancy, for he described that opening revue as 'A Crazy Week'.

Val Parnell had seen a revue called 'The Young Bloods' staged by Jimmy Nervo at the Nottingham Empire. Nervo, who came from a circus family, was a skilled acrobat, could ride bareback and had once been a member of a wire-walking act called the Four Holloways (Holloway being his real name). His partner Teddy Knox was a fine character actor who could also juggle. In addition to doing their own act, they used these skills in 'The Young Bloods' to intrude on everyone else's act, with hilarious effect. It was novel, it was new, and Parnell filed it away on a shelf in his memory, ready to dust down and present anew when the opportunity arose.

It came when two Palladium favourites, Glaswegians Charlie Naughton and Jimmy Gold, found themselves with a vacant date. They threatened to sign for a show with the rival Stoll circuit unless Parnell offered them work at the Palladium. Such was the paucity of good comedians that Parnell was unwilling to lose his two stars to a rival, yet how could he fit Naughton and Gold into a prepared Variety bill that already included two double acts?

One of the two acts already booked for the Palladium was Nervo and Knox. That's the answer, thought Parnell — instead of appearing as separate turns, let the double acts intrude on one another. 'Do anything you like. Use fair means or foul. But be sure to make the audience laugh,' were the instructions on opening night.

Husband-and-wife team Billy Caryll and Hilda Mundy were the third double act on the bill, and Eddie Gray, the phoney-French-talking juggler, was co-opted into the fun. The rest of the 'Crazy Week' bill comprised artists who offered the principals plenty of opportunity to 'get in on the act'.

The verdict of the London *Evening News* was: 'One of the funniest shows for a long time'. The plaudits encouraged Black to embark on a second 'Crazy Week' in December. Packed houses boosted his confidence still further, and a 'Crazy Month' was announced for June 1932. A fourth double act was added to the cast — Flanagan and Allen, already firm favourties at the Palladium, where they had made their first appearance as second turn on a bill headed by singer Peter Dawson. 'We were like children at a first party,' Bud Flanagan recalled later. The 'going home present' was a message from Black: 'Make that eight minutes of yours twelve minutes tomorrow.'

Those extra four minutes gave birth to a running gag forever to be associated with the Crazy Gang. 'We decided that if I muffed a word I would shout "Oi!",' said Bud. 'The orchestra would shout back "Oi!" and we hoped this would fill out the extra time.' In succeeding years every outrageous Flanagan pun — and there were thousands — was to get the 'Oi!' treatment.

	'All aboard'
Allen:	*'Wait a minute, you can't sail without us.'*
	'Oh, can't we? Who are all those kids, and who are you, anyway?'

120

Allen:	*'I'm Chesney Allen of the Crazy Gang. Mr. George Black is sending us on a cruise and he's put me in charge. And these kids, as you call them, are the rest of the Gang.'*
Flanagan:	*'Don't argue with him, Ches. Let's get a plank.'*
Allen:	*'A plank?'*
Flanagan:	*'A piece of wood.'*
Allen:	*'A piece of wood?'*
Gang:	*(in unison): 'A-board, a-board! Oi! Oi!'*

The son of a Polish Jew, Flanagan was born Robert Weinthrop on 14 October 1896 in a fish and chip shop off Whitechapel Road in the East End of London. Amongst the fish fryers, batter mixers and potato peelers, young Bud gave his first public performances — charging the neighbourhood kids a farthing for the privilege of seeing him perform his conjuring tricks. At fourteen, with a ha'penny in his pocket, Bud ran away from home. Or, rather, he walked — all the way to Southampton, where he talked his way aboard a ship by claiming to be an electrician's mate, and set sail for New York. He was selling newspapers outside a subway station when one of his regulars, a theatrical agent, asked him if he would like to play a bell-hop in a new play. He was paid twelve dollars a week for saying one line: 'This way, sir.'

Bud became infatuated with show business and teamed up with another youngster called Dale Burgess. They took their first faltering steps as a double act at a fleapit of a theatre in Philadelphia called The Gaiety.

When Britain went to war, Flanagan decided to return home and enlist. On the battlefield, in between fighting the Germans from a horse-drawn gun battery, he ran an army concert party — and, over egg and chips in a frowzy cafe close to the line at Passchendaele, he met Chesney Allen. He also met a six-foot sergeant major who gave him a particularly harassing time, passing every dangerous or unpleasant job his way. On the day he was transferred to another unit, Bud's parting words to the sergeant were, 'When this war is over I shall always remember you. I shall use your name on stage, you horrible bastard.' The sergeant's name was Flanagan.

The next occasion Bud met up with Chesney Allen, the latter was manager of the great music-hall artist Florrie Forde. Bud joined Florrie's company and he and Allen began doing spots together. When Florrie called down the curtain on her touring revue, Bud and Ches branched out on their own and were soon topping provincial Variety bills.

By the time Flanagan and Allen were added to the 'Crazy Month' cast, they had already played the Palladium and appeared in the 1932 Royal Variety Performance with Naughton and Gold and Nervo and Knox, the second pair performing a burlesque written by Flanagan. Nevertheless, the original 'Crazy Week' team were disturbed to learn that two interlopers had been invited to join the show, and made little effort to disguise their feelings. Flanagan pleaded with George Black to release him from the contract. 'Give it time,' Black urged. 'They're a decent bunch really.'

Flanagan and Allen could not have made a more conspicuous entrance. Black transported them from the Holborn Empire — where they had been appearing — to the Palladium in a huge cage perched on the back of a lorry. Every night the Gang greeted the customers in the foyer and during the intermission Flanagan put on a chef's hat and sold hot dogs from a trolley in the stalls.

On stage the humour was vulgar and violent, unrehearsed and uninhibited, boisterous and bawdy. Above all, it was *fun.* Fun the night juggler Bob Dupont was handed a ball which refused to bounce. Fun when Eddie Gray went on to perform his juggling act only to discover that the clubs had been smeared with Vaseline. Fun when Jimmy Nervo stuffed a couple of lighted cigarette ends in Charlie Naughton's hat and it caught fire midway through the scene. Fun when Bud Flanagan paraded on stage with a huge poster showing two eunuchs posted outside a harem door, and shouted: 'They're off!' Fun the night the Gang invited Irish heavyweight boxer Jack Doyle on stage to sing a chorus of 'Mother Macree', then, as he finished, gave him a glass of water, fanned him with a towel and carried him off on a stretcher. Fun when Stanley Holloway joined the Gang for a sketch in which he had to push Charlie Naughton on stage in a pram. Nobody told Holloway that the pram was loaded with weights.

However, the Crazy Gang's humour was not confined to the boards. Visiting their dressing-rooms was a perilous venture into the unknown. Flanagan had a pipe fixed which led round the wall from the wash basin, and was connected to a shower nozzle placed strategically over the dressing-room door. One night, however, it was Flanagan who got a drenching — someone had crept in during the day and drilled small holes along the length of the pipe.

A favourite trick was to slash into shreds the umbrella a visitor had unwisely left on the floor, replace it in its cover and contemplate the flood of invective that was certain to be unleashed on the next rainy day.

The most cleverly conceived of their backstage gags was the phoney radio set. Flanagan and Allen occupied a dressing-room adjoining one used by Nervo and Knox. A hole was drilled through the partition wall and a microphone in Bud Flanagan's room connected to a radio set in Jimmy Nervo's room. For most of the day the radio would be tuned in to the normal, Home, Light or Third programme of the BBC. But at the flick of a switch, Flanagan and Allen could break into any radio programme and continue with a fictitious broadcast of their own.

Among the many well-known visitors taken in by this piece of tomfoolery was George Jackley, father of the rubber-necked comedian Nat Jackley. The BBC were broadcasting a history of the Lyceum Theatre in London, where George had successfully played as a pantomime dame for a number of years. As he was at the Palladium that night, Jackley asked Nervo and Knox if he could listen to the broadcast on their radio. 'Certainly', they told him. Jackley was happily listening to the authentic broadcast when Bud Flanagan in the adjoining room flicked the switch, and Teddy Knox, a master of accents and dialects, took over the commentary.

'Nobody ever thinks of the Lyceum,' said Knox, 'without

recalling George Jackley.' The comedian sat up proudly in his chair, anticipating the compliments to follow. The 'commentator' continued, 'How this man ever got away with presenting such a load of rubbish for so long I will never know.' Poor Jackley almost burst a blood vessel as the slanderous commentary continued. Indeed, he was so completely taken in − and so angry − that he consulted a solicitor and threatened to sue the BBC, who were naturally at a loss to understand his complaint. Jackley was unconvinced even when he was shown the script used for the broadcast. 'You can't fool me,' he told the BBC. 'I was sitting in Jimmy Nervo's dressing-room. . .' Then the penny dropped.

Even members of the Gang were not immune from each other's practical jokes. When the lights dimmed at the close of one scene, the rest of the Gang leapt on Eddie Gray, pulled off every stitch of his clothing, and left him to streak through the corridors to his dressing-room as naked as the day he was born.

One macabre trick the Gang pulled still brings a chill to the Palladium old hands who fell victim to it. A scene in 'London Rhapsody' included a replica of the Chamber of Horrors at Madame Tussaud's. One of the life-size models was a sinister figure with a dark beard in the act of striking out with a dagger. Between shows the boys borrowed the figure and stood it in the ladies' toilet. Then they replaced the normal light with a blue bulb to create an eerie effect, and waited for the result. A succession of screams from the little room told them the horrification had worked.

Not surprisingly, the Crazy Gang's humour occasionally got out of hand and brought protests from George Black, whose authority was such that he was able to discipline six of the highest-paid performers in the land and still keep them working happily for him. If a gag offended him, Black would inquire, 'How did that one find its way into the show?' 'It just crept in, Guv'nor.' 'Well, see that it just creeps out again.'

'Each of the double acts was a little jealous of the others,' recalls Arthur Askey. 'Black was adept at playing one off against the other.' He remembers the night Eddie Gray went into the Royal Box and sat with his bare feet dangling over the front. Suddenly, while the rest of the Gang were performing on stage, Eddie let out a great guffaw — and a pair of false teeth dropped from his mouth. The audience roared with laughter as the teeth hung suspended on a thread from the box. Bud complained to George Black. Next day Eddie Gray was summoned to the office. 'Did you sit in the box last last night and dangle a set of false teeth over the stalls?' he was asked. 'Yes, I did, Guv'nor,' Eddie confessed. 'Good boy,' said Black. 'Keep it in.'

The success of the Crazy Gang shows led to a second 'Crazy Month' in September 1932, a third in November and, the following year, a 'Crazy Show' which ran for fourteen weeks.

A memorable marathon run of revues followed: 'Life Begins at Oxford Circus', 'Round About Regent Street', 'All Alight at Oxford Circus', 'O'Kay for Sound', 'London Rhapsody' — which opened in September 1937 and saw the collective name 'Crazy Gang' on a theatre poster for the first time — 'These Foolish Things', 'The Little Dog Laughed' and 'Top of the World'.

In the style of all great comics, the Crazy Gang could alternate comedy with pathos. Flanagan and Allen managed it with sentimental ballads like 'Strolling' and 'Underneath the Arches'. Noel Gay wrote 'Run Rabbit Run' for 'The Little Dog Laughed', Michael Carr and Jimmy Kennedy composed 'Hometown' for 'London Rhapsody'.

After the blitz had prematurely closed 'Top of the World', the Gang split up. In 1947 they re-formed, but without Chesney Allen, who had been forced by crippling rheumatism to retire from the stage. The Gang moved to a new residence — London's Victoria Palace. Twice nightly, for another fifteen years, they played to packed houses.

Jimmy Gold died in 1967 at the age of 81, Bud Flanagan a year later aged 72, Teddy Knox in 1974 aged 78, Jimmy Nervo in December 1975 aged 78 and Charlie Naughton in February 1976 aged 89.

'Goodbye — we're off to fresh adventures,
When somewhere they are certain to be found,

There's no need to be sad, for there's laughter to be had
If you only stop to look around.
And we're the ones who always seem to find it,
For we don't care a hang,
You can think that we are loopy, but we're not at making
whoopee,
We're the Palladium Crazy Gang.
Goodbye, customers!'

The Royal Family has little say in the selection of artists for the Royal Variety Performances, but King George VI and Queen Elizabeth repeatedly asked that the Crazy Gang be included on the bill. Today another double act is a firm favourite with the present Queen and Prince Philip: Morecambe and Wise.

Few artists are able to generate the warmth and affection that greet Eric Morecambe and Ernie Wise whenever they step onto a stage. But surprisingly, they have never been really at home playing the London Palladium. 'It probably stems from our first appearance with Ernie Ford in 1952,' says Morecambe. 'We had the shakes and didn't do too well. The Palladium gave us a quick return booking — for 1962. Another reason, I think, is that the theatre doesn't have footlights. I don't like to see an audience' — without the glare of the footlights it is possible to see the customers in the stalls — 'if I look down and see someone half asleep or reading a programme or lighting a cigarette when they are supposed to be laughing at my gags, that upsets me.'

Their most disastrous Palladium appearance was on a live Sunday night television show. Everything went wrong. Morecambe was ill and had to be given injections before he could go on; a complicated sketch using a number of props, visual effects and the theatre's trap door, went totally awry; and words were exchanged with a heckler in the audience. As the comics walked off to lukewarm applause, Morecambe turned to Wise and said, 'I should imagine that's the worst bloody act we've ever done.' Back from the audience came an emphatic 'Yes!' Morecambe had forgotten he was wearing a radio microphone — his off-stage remark had carried to everyone in the theatre that night.

Morecambe and Wise were a couple of fourteen-year-olds when they met for the first time in 1940 as two of Bryan Michie's 'Discoveries'. They toured the country in a show called 'Youth Takes a Bow'. Morecambe, the shorter one in those days, appeared as a gormless kid in cut-down tail coat held together with an enormous safety pin, short evening-suit trousers and red socks, a kiss curl over one eye, huge spectacles, and sucking a lollipop.

By comparison Wise was a sophisticated West End performer. He had already appeared at the Palladium with Arthur Askey and Richard Murdoch in Jack Hylton's 'Band Waggon', and was being hailed as the next Jack Buchanan. 'Railway porter's son a star overnight,' read the headlines. He came on without a sign of nerves, full of Yorkshire cockiness,' wrote one reviewer. 'He sang in a voice that made microphones unnecessary; cracked a pair of North Country jokes; and did a whirlwind step dance with terrific aplomb and efficiency. He is a sort of Yorkshire Max Miller, tilts his battered bowler over one eye and has a wicked wink.' But Wise's brash, confident exterior masked a basic shyness that he retains to this day. 'Even then, entertaining was a sort of personality prop which helped me cover up a deep-rooted sense of inadequacy', he says. 'The moment I put on my comedy suit I was able to step out of my very private little world and be an entirely different person, a cheeky chappie.'

When 'Youth Takes a Bow' opened at the New Theatre, Oxford, Wise found himself walking the blacked-out streets in a fruitless search for lodgings. He tapped on a lodging house door. The landlady was apologetic. She already had 'two or three people from the theatre, you see'. The 'people from the theatre' turned out to be Eric Morecambe and his mother, Sadie Bartholomew, who told the landlady that he could share Eric's bed. Ernie Wise stayed on as a permanent paying guest, and a new double act was born. It was Sadie who persuaded the pair to team up. 'Our style was very much

Abbott and Costello,' recalls Wise. 'We used to talk with American accents: "Whaddya gonna do now, Morecambe?" "I'll tell ya somefing, Wise." It was terrible!'

When Jimmy Jewel and Ben Warriss split up in 1967 after thirty years together, Jewel said, 'It's a funny thing about double acts. It's a bit like a marriage. You start off as struggling youngsters in Oldham sharing the same bed, work your way steadily to the top, become more prosperous and swap the bed for a hotel room. Then, suddenly, you find you have drifted apart. You don't even share the same dressing-room. Ben and I never had a cross word. There was no row — but we knew it was time to part.' Morecambe and Wise are only too aware of the dangers. Professionally there is an empathy between them. Socially, 'We are two entirely different personalities,' says Wise. 'Ernie has never been to my house, and I have never been to his.'

Morecambe and Wise always finish their act with a 'question time' session with the audience. Without fail the first three questions are: 'How's Luton Town doing?', 'Does Ernie really wear a wig?' and 'Show us your short, fat, hairy legs'. There is always a wag who will crack a gag of his own: 'My mother-in-law nearly went to Morecambe for her holidays. But she got Wise and stayed at home.' And always Morecambe will comment: 'It's time to go — the audience is becoming funnier than us.' The 'question time' idea was cribbed from Ed Sullivan's television show in the United States. The first time Morecambe and Wise attempted it in Britain, it was a disaster. 'Any questions?' invited Morecambe. The audience sat in stony silence. 'Anyone want to ask us anything?' Not a word. Finally, after a long and embarrassing pause, a lone voice piped up. 'Do you think mopeds should be allowed on the motorways?'

There's no answer to that.

One night at the Palladium the act that preceded theirs on the bill over-ran its time, and Morecambe and Wise were asked to cut their spot by two minutes. As they had been allocated only eight minutes anyway, it meant losing a quarter of the act, but being two of the most disciplined comics in the business, the boys acceded to the request. It was six minutes of misery. The audience hardly raised a titter. The comedian who followed them on the bill over-ran *his* time by half as much again, and went off to a tremendous ovation.

'From that moment, we thought sod 'em,' says Morecambe. 'The next time we were on the show and were asked to take two minutes out, Ernie and I looked at each other, gave a nod and said, "Fine, fine." Then we went out and *added* two minutes — and we paralysed 'em.'

An admirer of the Crazy Gang as performers, Eric Morecambe holds strong views about their backstage tomfoolery. Wasn't it funny when they sabotaged artists' props? Wasn't it funny when they nailed dancers' shoes to the stage? 'No,' insists Morecambe. 'That wasn't funny. For someone to come on half-way through your act and ruin the sketch for you just isn't funny. And if somebody did it in our show, they would never work with us again — even if it got a big laugh.'

But even Morecambe and Wise have been known to pull a few 'harmless' tricks at the Palladium, as property master Ron Harris knows to his cost. Like most of the backstage staff, he has often been called upon to act as an 'extra' to a performer on stage — removing a microphone, a discarded garment or an unwanted prop. But one evening he was surprised when Morecambe and Wise asked him to put on full stage make-up. He spent twenty minutes assiduously applying rouge, powder and colouring. Throughout the show he stood in the wings awaiting his big moment. In the middle of Morecambe and Wise's act, Harris was called on. This was it: his big scene. It lasted precisely five seconds — just long enough to walk on, be the butt of one of their jokes, and walk off again. The joke was doubly on him.

It was a tense and historic night at the London Palladium. The longest-running show in the theatre's history, 'Happy and Glorious', had just come off; George Black had died, and his successor Val Parnell was presenting his first Palladium production. The eyes of the entertainment industry were focused on London's most famous theatre. As Black's number two,

Parnell had gained the respect of the profession, but this night in May 1946 was to be the supreme test of his worthiness to assume the mantle of the master showman.

As the curtain was about to rise, Parnell left his seat in the stalls and walked through the pass door to the stage. The two performers on whom Parnell had staked his reputation were waiting nervously in the wings. In appearance they could hardly have been more of a contrast: one lugubrious, wide-mouthed, thin-lipped, a toupee covering his balding head; the other dapper, beak-nosed, with protruding ears and shoe-black, brilliantined hair. The only similarity was the look of anxiety on their faces. They had achieved success in the provinces, but never before had Jimmy Jewel and Ben Warriss topped a Palladium bill.

The relationship between Parnell and Jewel was closer than that of showman and star: Jimmy Jewel was Parnell's godson. The boss took him to one side, put his arm round his shoulder, and said, 'Look, Jimmy. Nobody is worried but you.'

These encouraging words gave Jewel and Warriss just the fillip they needed. The show, 'High Time', was a huge success, the stars were booked for a radio series called 'Up the Pole', and a new show business horizon opened for them.

Not that 'High Time' was without incident. One of the co-stars was 'Two Ton' Tessie O'Shea. Parnell had decided that, being a big lady, she required a big entrance. Jumbo-sized, in fact. Tessie made her entrance sitting astride an elephant. It was a new experience for her. Not being as well-versed in the art of elephant-riding as Sabu, Tessie promptly fell off, and for several weeks she was out of the show.

Backstage was like a menagerie. In addition to the elephant, the show also had a horse, which Jewel and Warriss used in a gag about the Derby: 'Not only did we back the winner — we bought it. And here it is. . .' On stage would walk a great lumbering shire horse. The joke always brought a big laugh. It was the only part the animal played in the show, but it got into such a routine that at 5 pm every Sunday — when there was no performance — it would charge about in its stable and kick frantically at the door, as if to tell its owner, 'Hey, come

130

on. I'm late for my starring role at the Palladium.'

Some nights a stand-in horse had to be used, and that would guarantee the biggest laugh of the show. 'Not being used to the theatre, as soon as the animal saw the lights and heard the music it would become frightened,' says Jewel. 'The horse would react in the most natural way possible — and do its business on the stage. Mind, it could have been worse — it might have been the elephant.'

In 1950 Jewel and Warriss were back at the Palladium as robbers in the pantomime 'Babes in the Wood'. One of their props was an amazing Model-T Ford car. The wonder-car did everything. Using twenty-five pedals, Jewel could make doors fly off, the back drop out, explosions occur — and even send the vehicle round in circles without using the steering wheel. By the skilful employment of a windscreen wiper motor and a series of camshafts, Jimmy could make the car start and stop by remote control.

The contraption terrified Parnell, who always looked the other way when the boys were working it on stage. One night his worst fears were realised. Warriss accidentally kicked a pedal as he clambered out of the car. The thing shot forward, tore across the stage, and knocked all the scenery down.

For another appearance at the Palladium, the boys used material belonging to Abbott and Costello. However, it was all quite legitimate. George Black had seen Abbott and Costello in the States and decided that one of their sketches was right for Jewel and Warriss. He paid the Americans £250 and offered the sketch to Jimmy and Ben for the same price. Not having reached the top salary bracket, Jewell and Warriss reluctantly told the Guv'nor they could not afford the material. 'All right,' said Black. 'Give me £25 a week until it's paid for.' Jewel and Warriss must have been the first comics to crack gags which they had bought on the 'never-never'!

Jewel and Warriss also had the distinction of standing-in for Laurel and Hardy when Stan Laurel was taken ill on a visit to London. Oliver Hardy introduced the boys on stage, and stayed to watch their act.

Nothing, however, was going to force Stan Laurel to miss one of the proudest moments of his show-business life — the 1947 Royal Variety Performance at the Palladium. And nobody watched Stan's and Ollie's act with more interest than their co-stars on that royal bill — The Crazy Gang.

Top of the Bill

'It's impossible, tell the sun to leave the sky, it's just impossible.' On the stage at the London Palladium an 'unmistakable' voice is crooning into the microphone. In a distant office, a Palladium executive turns up the volume on the theatre's Tannoy system. Pressmen, tipped off that the star has arrived, hurry to the theatre. Attendants and cleaners in the auditorium interrupt their chores to catch a glimpse of this world-famous entertainer.

The Magic Moment has arrived. Or has it?

In the foyer, a handsome man in his mid-sixties — greying hair, gold-rimmed spectacles, overcoated against the chill November night — is being escorted on a tour of the Palladium. 'It's one hell of a time to be rehearsing,' he jokes, glancing at his watch, which shows a little after midnight.

'It's impossible, ask a baby not to cry, it's just impossible.' The voice drifting through the loudspeakers sounds uncannily like Perry Como's. Yet the man in the foyer is Perry Como. The man singing on stage is his stand-in. His name is Ray Charles — not the famous singer, but Como's choral director. He is as familiar with the numbers and the performance as the artist himself. 'Could we have the auditorium lights up?' he asks. 'Mr. Como likes to see the audience.'

Why does Perry Como not rehearse himself? 'I don't need to,' he says. 'I leave all that to the band and Ray. I just want to make sure the orchestra sounds right, that's all.' He returns to his hotel without setting one foot on stage. Even at the final run-through next day, he rehearses only part of his act.

It is all part of the trappings of a superstar. And this chapter is all about superstars — the biggest names in show business who have topped the bill at the Palladium.

Hermione Gingold once received a beautifully-written letter from a young girl asking if she could guide her through the first faltering steps of a show-business career. Miss Gingold was so moved by the letter that she invited the girl to her apartment and asked her which branch of the business she was interested in. 'Oh, I don't care,' the girl replied. 'I just want to be a star.'

The show business adage that stars are born and not made is only true in part. To reach the top, they say, takes fifty per cent luck and fifty per cent hard work. The hit record or the plum rôle; a clever gimmick dreamed up by a skilful publicity machine; a diligent manager and a far-sighted agent — these are the bricks a performer builds on to reach the top. But only talent keeps him there.

Superstars are something different again. They possess that indefinable something — a charisma that far outshines the rest — that earns them vast fortunes and ensures a countless band of devotees wherever they perform. Not all were superstars when they first played the Palladium. For many, it was an appearance at the world's number one Variety theatre that established their reputation, as in the case of Danny Kaye.

However, one young American brought over by Parnell found that his fame had preceded him. The hell-raising days were a thing of the future, and young Blue Eyes was in London for the first time — but it was a hostile Press that greeted him. Sinatra was billed as 'The Voice', but few British critics took his singing seriously. Fleet Street was preoccupied with his romance with Ava Gardner, who just happened to be filming in Britain the same month. Sinatra was furious that reporters were only interested in his love life. When a cameraman tried to photograph the couple together, Sinatra lost his temper —

a foretaste of the many skirmishes with photographers that were to follow. While the Press may have concentrated their attention on Miss Gardner, Sinatra's was centred on his two-week engagement at the London Palladium. He was meticulous in rehearsal, patiently briefing the musicians to the extent of running through the arrangements bar by bar.

It was a lean and hungry-looking Frank Sinatra who walked onto a London stage for the first time on 10 July 1950. Though his dinner jacket patently never came from Savile Row, his music had style woven into every note. His fifteen songs included 'Ol' Man River', the soliloquy from 'Carousel' and — in response to the first night audience's demands — 'Nancy', a song dedicated to the wife he had parted from.

The *Daily Express* reported that nobody swooned, but the singer was certainly mobbed. On the opening day the 'fifties equivalent of the teenyboppers were on parade outside the stage door at 10 am. They carried balloons bearing the name 'Frankie' and home-made banners proclaiming 'Sinatrally Yours.' A great squeal of delight greeted Sinatra's arrival. 'Grinning widely, hatless, entirely unruffled, the bow-tied bantam was through the fans in five seconds flat,' the newspapers reported. An eighteen-year-old girl handed him a red carnation. The bow tie was lost in a mêlée of eager hands. After the show, huge crowds gathered in Argyll Street. New words adorned the banners: 'Thanks, Val Parnell, we knew he'd be swell.' Sinatra waved, and went off to a party with Ava Gardner.

In 1950 the best seat in the house to see Sinatra cost just fifteen shillings. A seat in the upper circle was half a crown. In November 1975 when Sinatra made a return visit to the Palladium, the prices had risen to fifteen guineas and £3.50 respectively. Not that there was any shortage of takers: all seats for the one-week appearance were snapped up in hours. The Palladium took on the appearance of a fortress. Nobody, but nobody, was allowed backstage without a special Sinatra identity card, and stage hands were warned not to pass the superstar's door. Outside the theatre the singer's comings and goings were reminiscent of scenes from *The Godfather.* Each time Sinatra's green Daimler pulled to a halt a posse of beefy Italian-American bodyguards would jump to attention and surround the car.

At rehearsals a 'No Smoking' order went out to the musicians. Since he broke the fifty-a-day habit, Sinatra cannot tolerate smoking anywhere near him. In 1950 Sinatra had sipped tea between the songs; in 1975 the liquid refreshment came neat from a glass.

'You've had lollipops here' — a reference to the Royal Variety Show appearance of Telly Savalas, star of 'Kojak', 'and milk-drinking Burton, but I'm here now and it's gonna be booze and broads and all that stuff,' he told the audience.

The welcome Sinatra received was nothing to the near-hysteria that greeted the first appearance in Britain of another American singer — the 'Prince of Wails', Johnnie Ray. The ballyhoo that preceded his arrival in March 1953 made Sinatra's publicity look like a Women's Institute hand-out.

By his own admission, Ray's greatest asset was his ability to cry in public. By the time he reached the Palladium, the twenty-five year old singer had shot from obscurity to become the hottest single property in the United States. The son of a paper-mill worker, Ray was the unlikeliest of sex symbols. Gaunt in appearance and with defective hearing that required him to wear a hearing aid, he could reduce girls to shrieking hysteria at the drop of a tear.

Americans were divided over the new heart-throb. One New York journalist complained that his paper should have sent a sociologist to review Ray's act, not a theatre critic. Another suggested that his success was a sad reflection on the human race. But Tallullah Bankhead told the world, 'I'm going to adopt him,' and Ava Gardner admitted, 'He sends me.' To which Sinatra sarcastically retorted, 'In what direction?'

Ray was immune to the criticisms. Earning £2,500 a week, he could afford to be. 'Man, there's one thing I'm smart enough to realise. I have no talent. I still sing as flat as a billiard table. They can knock my voice, but they've got to admit I'm a showman.'

That at least was true. The lingering end to his songs was quite something to behold. Rising from the piano on the last note Ray would rotate one arm like a windmill, raise it high into the air, sink on one knee and take a long, low, bow. 'There is no hope or cheer in anything he does', mused one critic after seeing him at the Palladium. 'He is startling and disturbing.' He delivered all his hit records — like 'Cry' (which sold almost two million), 'The Little White Cloud that Cried,' and 'Tell the Lady I Said Goodbye' — with a pained expression and tears in his eyes.

If it was agony on stage, it was ecstasy in the stalls. Hysterical shrieks greeted Ray's first venture onto the Palladium stage. Girls swooned and cried. Girls pulled at their hair — and at each other's. Girls tore at their clothes. 'Cry, Johnnie, cry,' they screamed.

He played out of rhythm, he sang off-key. In the middle of one number he stopped and confessed, 'I've run out of lyrics.' *The Stage* wrote, 'With my raincoat firmly buttoned up to the neck I sat in the front stalls and waited for the tears to cascade. As an honest critic, I must report that I did not get a teeny bit wet. I fancied I saw a trickle at the end. But perhaps my neighbour was right. "Don't you believe it," he said. "It's perspiration." '

Night after night the young worshippers paid homage. Ray had to change his hotel continually because managers objected to hordes of girls camping in the street outside, playing his hits on portable record players. Backstage at the Palladium there were shades of James Bond as the staff plotted the singer's nightly escape route. One night they dressed him in a brown overall and cloth cap and got him to carry the back end of a piece of scenery that was being loaded on a waiting van. On another occasion Errol Flynn was fed to the screaming fans at the back door, while Johnnie Ray made a speedy exit at the front. Unfortunately, a few eagle-eyed girls spotted him, and pounced on the singer's taxi. In a panic, the driver

137

accelerated away with the youngsters still clinging to the cab. Though they were thrown into the road and needed the attentions of a nurse, they found a few bruises a small price to pay for getting so close to their idol.

The army of fans grew until an estimated two thousand were thronging round the stage door. The girls had travelled to London from every corner of the country, some even throwing in their jobs to make the trip. The Palladium management ordered the heavy main gates to be closed and locked with iron bars. Again and again the chanting mob charged the doors. Some of the youngsters were literally banging their heads against the woodwork. All of a sudden there was a tremendous crash. A great roar went up — the fans had broken through, and the theatre crew retreated to their second line of defence, the stage door. Bolts were hastily secured, and in seconds a mass of wild, tear-stained faces were pressing against the windows.

Johnnie Ray was locked in his dressing-room. The police were called and fought a desperate battle to push the fans back outside the main gates. Someone noticed that a girl had fainted right outside the stage door and was in danger of being trampled to death. The door was opened just sufficiently to drag her inside. A friend was ushered in to look after her. The youngster showed no sign of coming round: she was out for the count. Her friend was leaning over her when Johnnie Ray popped his head round the corner. The second girl looked up, saw the singer — and fainted as well.

Ray returned the following year with a new song called 'Such a Night'. To date he has made nine appearances at the Palladium, including the 1955 Royal Variety Performance.

Years later, he recalled those frenetic days: 'I was pretty screwed up,' he said. 'For years I was surrounded by people I hated. There was no one I could trust or confide in. I lived on my nerves until they were raw. I would sit in hotel rooms, literally sweating with terror. And to escape from my nightmares I'd run to the nearest bar and get stoned. In ten years I made a million pounds, and I was the unhappiest guy in the world — erratic, undependable and isolated.'

138

In 1976 Ray returned to the Palladium on a nostalgic bill that included Billy Daniels, Frances Faye and The Ink Spots. His fans had not forgotten him. Within a day of Ray's visit being announced, one admirer had purchased £150 worth of tickets.

Ten years passed and the fans in seamed stockings, tight sweaters and pencil-slim skirts gave way to a new generation of teenyboppers. The focus of their attention was not a lean young man, but four healthy-looking youths with mop-heads and pulsating guitars.

On 13 October 1963, John, Paul, George and Ringo — the new pop phenomenon from Merseyside — came to London and the Palladium. Ten months before they had been unknown. Now they were earning £10,000 a year, and the Liverpool sound had carried south with sufficient impact to guarantee them a hot reception. By 10 am the streets outside the Palladium were packed with several hundred fans — many dressed in sweaters emblazoned with the Beatles' heads.

The boys had a rehearsal at 11 am. But it was obvious that smuggling them into the building would be no easy task. At the appointed time, two limousines drew up outside the theatre — then accelerated away again. Fifteen minutes later the cars came back; but if anything, the crowd had grown. The Beatles made another hasty retreat.

Backstage the telephone rang. 'Can you help us?' pleaded Brian Epstein, the Beatles' manager. 'We're in Wardour Street. Our driver has passed the stage door twice. If he stops, we'll be torn to pieces.' Stage doorkeeper George Cooper suggested a decoy plan: one limousine, minus the Beatles, was to drive up to the stage door; a second car, also empty, would drive up to the front entrance. 'I'll arrange for two taxis to pick you up', said George. 'Get the boys to lie flat on the floor of the cabs, and the drivers will pull up at a secret entrance away from the fans.'

Six hefty stagehands were assigned to meet the taxis. The ruse worked — but still the crowd grew. By mid-day more than a hundred police were on duty outside the Palladium.

Imprisoned by their fans, the four young men settled down in their dressing-room to a Sunday lunch of roast beef and Yorkshire pudding, while messengers delivered piles of autograph books, letters and gifts.

During the afternoon a group of fifty youngsters forced their way through the gates. The Palladium staff were ready for the onslaught. They grabbed the fire hoses from the wall and aimed them menacingly at the crowd. But while the water battle was being played out below, a second group of fans were searching for another way in — via the roof.

The performance itself went off without incident, but there was still the problem of getting the four lads safely out again. A stage door departure was out of the question. It had to be the front entrance. The foyer was cleared and the police formed a cordon across Argyll Street. 'Get your boys out immediately,' ordered a police inspector. 'I can't expect my men to hold back the crowds for more than three minutes.' As the four climbed into the car, the police barrier broke. But too late — the Beatles had got away.

That night at the London Palladium give the English language a new word: Beatlemania.

Albert Locke, one of the producers of 'Sunday Night at the London Palladium', remembers an appearance of another leading pop group, the Rolling Stones. The Stones had been hesitant about accepting the invitation for the show, unsure whether the sound they created in the recording studio could be faithfully reproduced in the vast auditorium of the Palladium. But, finally, they agreed.

'They were late for rehearsal,' says Locke. 'When they did arrive we had all the grumbles — they can't hear this, they couldn't do that. But after a great struggle we got through.'

The time came to rehearse the finale. By tradition the Sunday Palladium show ended with the artists waving goodbye as the stage revolved. Locke was passed a message from the Stones. They refused to join the others on the revolving stage. Locke was furious. When the group walked to the side of the stage he turned on them. 'Who do you think you are?' he stormed. 'How dare you insult the London Palladium and the rest of the cast? Get off the bloody stage!'

What Locke had not realised was that the Press were taking photographs of the whole scene. Next morning the Palladium row was splashed across the newspapers. 'I don't think any other artist — not even the greatest of international stars — ever refused to appear on the revolving stage,' says Locke.

No sooner had the curtain come down on the performance than the Stones were smuggled away through a side door into a cab to escape the waiting fans. Unfortunately one of the policemen assigned to give the group a helping hand was a little over-zealous — along with the Rolling Stones, he bundled into the waiting cab an elderly gentleman who just happened to be passing — and the taxi drove off with the poor fellow hanging out of the window loudly protesting that he had been kidnapped.

The fans dream up some extraordinary tricks to meet their idols at the Palladium, but one girl was prepared to go further than most. She called a press conference to announce publicly that she was engaged to Cliff Richard, and, according to the newspaper reports, had put up the banns at a church in Kilburn, London, and posted off more than a hundred wedding invitations.

Richard was dumbfounded when he arrived at the theatre and was shown a copy of the evening paper with the picture and story on the front page. 'What wedding?' he protested. 'I don't even know the girl.'

The Palladium staff knew her only too well; she was one of the stage door regulars. Often she would mingle with the crowds outside telling them she was appearing in the current show. If anyone asked her why she wasn't on stage, she would say that she had just popped out for a breath of fresh air. To prove the truth of her words, she would invite people to visit the box office and collect free tickets reserved in the name of her act, 'Candy the Cat'. Scores of people were taken in by her. They would turn up to demand free tickets, insisting, 'Candy sent us.'

During the run of the pantomime 'Cinderella' a few years ago, Richard, playing Buttons, was given a tear-jerking line to speak before his closing number. 'The Ugly Sisters have gone off with the broker's men, Cinderella has found her Prince, but what about me?' Carried away, a little girl ran from her seat to the front of the stalls and shouted, 'I'll marry you, Cliff!' There was scarcely a dry eye in the house.

One artist guaranteed to send his audience wild is Tom Jones, the singer from South Wales. His weeks at the Palladium are always a sell-out, bar takings soar, and there is always a crowd of celebrities in his dressing-room. His preparations for a performance have been likened to a boxer's training routine: he drinks only moderately, breakfasts on steak and eggs, works out in his own gymnasium and insists on a daily massage and sauna. 'The shows I do every night — twice a night at the Palladium — are as physically demanding as a fight,' Jones says.

Certainly those swivelling hips, those electrifying body movements, those X-certificate trousers, spell sex wherever he appears. It is no secret that women fall like ninepins for his masculine charms, often throwing articles of underwear onto the stage. On one occasion a woman climbed up on stage and unbuttoned her blouse. She had nothing on underneath. Not to be outdone, a second girl let her hot pants slip down. It is to prevent such sensational happenings that attendants always patrol the front of the orchestra pit for Jones's visits to the Palladium. But even that thin blue line has been broken.

Engelbert Humperdinck became an overnight sensation after his first appearance at the Palladium. The late Dickie Valentine — once a call-boy at the theatre — was booked for a Sunday television show, but at the last moment a throat infection forced him to cancel the engagement. Half-a-dozen artists were suggested as replacements, but Albert Locke plumped for a young man who had recently changed his name from Jerry Dorsey and climbed to the top of the charts with a record called 'Release Me'. Moments after Humperdinck finished his spot, the backstage telephone rang — just a viewer offering her congratulations. The phone rang again —

and again — and again. Not just the public, but the country's top entertainers as well, were ringing in to praise the newcomer.

His good fortune on that first appearance deserted him in 1974. He was in his dressing-room watching the other acts in the show on his television, when the screen went blank. 'I heard somebody shout that there was a bomb, and we had two minutes to clear the theatre,' he recalls. 'I couldn't believe it at first. I went to the side of the stage to check if it was all a hoax. But instead of compère Jim Dale at the microphone, there were two policemen with loud hailers telling the audience to get out at once.' The police gave the all-clear after thirty minutes, but it was too late to save the show.

Another bomb scare nearly ruined the sensational first live appearance in Britain of that vivacious, urchin-faced Hollywood star, Shirley MacLaine. A celebrity-studded audience packed the theatre for her opening night in February 1976. As they returned to their seats after the intermission, the star was nervously making her way along the narrow corridor leading from her dressing-room to the side of the stage. In the wings, two stagehands were deep in whispered conversation. 'There's been a bomb warning,' said one. 'We've been told not to say anything to Miss MacLaine.' But Shirley, only a few feet away, overheard the remark.

The alarm had been raised by an observant attendant who had spotted an attaché case beneath one of the empty seats at the front of the stalls. Police hurried to the theatre. The telephone warning, they learned, had not included the IRA codeword that had become the harbinger of a spate of bombings in London. In the opinion of the police, the call was a hoax. But the decision to clear the theatre or not was left to Palladium chairman Sir Lew Grade. He puffed for a moment at a huge Havana cigar and then decided: 'The show goes on!'

Shirley MacLaine could only guess at the drama out front as her name was announced and she ran onto the Palladium stage for the first time to sing her opening number. 'If They

Could See Me Now'. 'The song couldn't have been more appropriate,' she said later. 'After hearing that bomb warning I stood at the side of the stage shaking. Thank goodness the audience couldn't see me then!'

The attaché case turned out to be harmless — it belonged to a couple who stayed just a little too long in the bar.

The invitation to Shirley MacLaine to play the Palladium was in itself something of a surprise. The last occasion Shirley had worked for Lew Grade — on a disastrous television series — she had walked out on him and caught the first available plane back to New York. The newspapers made great play of 'a feud' between the impresario and the star. But in her Palladium dressing-room it was all very chummy. 'When we get to the party tonight you and I will Charleston together on a table top,' she told Sir Lew. Though somehow they never did quite get round to it, although the party went on well into the early hours.

Like Engelbert Humperdinck, Val Doonican was another singer to find himself famous overnight after a Sunday night Palladium show. He, too, had been in the business for a number of years without making it to the top.

Doonican patronised the same Soho barber as Palladium boss Val Parnell. As the barber clipped away at Parnell's hair he recounted the praise he had heard for Doonican's act. Alec Fine, chief booker for Associated Television, took Parnell to see the singer at a club in Manchester, they liked what they saw, booked Doonican for a second-from-top spot in their show — and his reputation was made. His relaxed style — perched on a stool as he strummed a guitar — his Irish charm, and a voice reminiscent of Jim Reeves, captivated the audience. 'Parnell booked me for the same spot the following week,' he remembers. 'Offers of work poured in, and my earnings trebled.'

One superstar who consistently eluded the Palladium management was Bing Crosby. In his early days, he was booked to appear as a member of the singing trio, The Rhythm Boys, but the singers cancelled their contract after another American vocal group had been given a cool recep-

Perry Como and his stand-in, Ray Charles, are introduced to the Queen Mother, 1974

(Doug McKenzie)

Frank Sinatra, Ella Fitzgerald and Count Basie, 1975

(Terry O'Neill)

The Palladium under siege during Johnnie Ray's vist, 1953

(ATV)

The Beatles backstage with Alma Cogan

ommy Steele on his 38th birthday,
974, after the opening night of 'Hans
Andersen'

(Sun)

Bob Hope on the Palladium stage

(Moss Empires)

Judy Garland rehearses for the 1957 Royal Variety Show

Michael Crawford, Harry Secombe, Telly Savalas and Vera Lynn, stars of the 1975 Royal Variety Show

(Su

tion at the theatre. 'We tried to entice him many times,' says Palladium producer Albert Knight. 'But he always turned us down.' However, the 'Old Groaner' did make an unscheduled appearance: 'Bing's great buddy Bob Hope had a gag in which a surprise personality would walk on in the middle of his act carrying a bottle of medicine and a spoon,' says Knight. 'Bob would halt his act, swallow the medicine, lick the spoon and carry on as if the interruption had never happened. Any celebrity who was in town would be inveigled into bringing on the medicine. The gag raised a laugh and the audience got a kick out of spotting the identity of the celebrity. They could hardly believe their eyes that night at the Palladium when the celebrity turned out to be Bing.'

Later in the show Crosby walked on again. An apron was tied round his middle and he was pushing a broom. While Hope joked, Crosby swept. The irony was not lost on Albert Knight. No amount of money could entice Bing to sing at the Palladium — but he was happy to sweep the stage for nothing.

In June 1976 Crosby finally relented. At the age of seventy-one, and after fifty years in show business, he agreed to appear at the Palladium for two weeks, as a 'thank you' gesture to his British fans. But he insisted that no seat should cost more than £5, and he donated his entire fee to charity.

Life backstage often belies the glamour and laughter and the brave front presented on stage.

'Who killed the starmaker?' was the question posed in the newspaper headlines one morning in May 1974. Edwin Thornley, personal stage director to Tommy Steele and the man behind many hit shows, had been found stabbed to death on Hungerford Bridge, which spans the Thames at Charing Cross. Two weeks earlier Thornley had returned to Britain after a triumphant tour of Canada with Frankie Vaughan in 'The Palladium Show'. Only hours before his death Thornley was backstage at the theatre chatting with Vaughan, who was now starring in a London version of the same show. Saying that he was going out front to watch the show, Thornley left the dressing-room. That was the last Vaughan ever saw of his friend. Thornley was heading for Waterloo Station when he was attacked and knifed in the throat.

Vaughan was shattered by the news, so much so that he lost his voice. That night he struggled through his act, but it was three days before his voice was fully restored.

Tommy Steele offered a £1,000 reward for information leading to the arrest of the killers. It transpired that Thornley, a homosexual, was the victim of a gang of 'queer bashers'. He was lured from Piccadilly Circus to Hungerford Bridge, stabbed, and robbed. In December 1974 one of the youths responsible was jailed for murder and his two accomplices convicted of manslaughter.

'The show must go on' is a hackneyed phrase, perhaps, but the sentiment is taken very seriously by the profession, nonetheless. During an appearance at the Palladium of French singing star Sacha Distel, his father was taken gravely ill. This was reported in the newspapers and hundreds of letters flooded into the theatre daily expressing sympathy and wishing his father a speedy recovery. At the close of the second house on the first Saturday of his two-week engagement, Distel flew home to France. The following day his father died. On Monday Distel was back at the Palladium in time for the first house, and insisted on completing his booking. The news of his father's death was kept from the Press, and even the singer's dash home for the funeral later that week went unreported.

The most difficult moments came at the end of each evening's performance, when the fans called backstage for Distel's autograph and gave him their good wishes for his father's recovery.

One tragic event did succeed in stopping the show: the shooting of Senator Robert Kennedy in June 1968. Sammy Davis Jnr. was appearing at the Palladium in the musical 'Golden Boy'. Twice he missed performances with laryngitis. When he read of the shooting of his close friend, Davis announced that he was too upset to appear that night. The rest of the cast were displeased, fearing that the show might be taken off permanently if he failed yet again to make an appearance. Leading lady Gloria De Haven led the revolt: she refused to go on stage without the star. Meanwhile Davis was brooding in his dressing-room and the audience waited patiently in the auditorium. The musical's American management suspended Miss De Haven on the spot, and she immediately burst into tears. Eventually the curtain went up half-an-hour late. Reporters and photographers, sensing that Davis might not appear, had gathered in the foyer. Now that he was actually on stage, they dispersed back to Fleet Street.

Then came the bombshell. During the intermission, Davis told the audience he could not continue. It was the signal for a mass exodus, and a stream of customers headed for the box office to demand their money back. The next day, 6 June, Kennedy died. A notice was posted outside the theatre stating that the charity performance planned for that night had been cancelled as a mark of respect for the dead Senator.

'Golden Boy' never fully recovered from those early setbacks. During the season a threat was made to Davis's life. Strict security measures were put into force backstage, and the West End Central police provided him with a personal bodyguard — a 6 feet 4 inch, seventeen-stone muscleman known as 'Nosher' Powell. While in London Davis rented a penthouse at the Playboy Club. His visitor one evening was Michael X, at that time leader of the British Black Power movement. Sammy asked 'Nosher' to collect some ice cubes from his room for the drinks. As he was returning, the policeman noticed a hefty-looking black gentleman lurking in the corridor. Without waiting to ask questions, 'Nosher' grabbed the fellow by the shoulder, spun him round and landed a vicious left hook on his jaw. The man sank to the floor, unconscious. Alarmed by the commotion outside, Davis and his guest rushed into the corridor. 'What happened?' asked Davis. The bodyguard explained. 'You idiot,' shouted Michael X. 'The man you hit is *my* bodyguard!'

'Nosher' Powell would have been a handy person to have around the night six sinister-looking characters turned up at

151

the stage door during an appearance by the American singer Billy Daniels. They looked for all the world like the archetypal heavies in a James Cagney movie. 'Go to Daniels' room,' the heavies' spokesman ordered the stage doorkeeper, George Cooper. 'Tell Jack Como some *friends* are here to see him.'

Cooper knew that the fellow was referring to the singer's guest that night, better known as Jack Spot, one-time self-styled king of London's underworld. Cooper's knees were quaking, but he gathered his thoughts quickly enough to blurt out. 'I can't do that. The show has started. Mr Daniels is on stage and his room is empty.' The 'heavy' growled. An ugly zig-zag scar down one side of his face made him appear even more menacing. 'All right. We'll be back when the show finishes,' he threatened.

The stage doorkeeper had not been exactly truthful. Billy Daniels was in his room. Told about his unwelcome guest, Daniels asked for a taxi to meet him at the front entrance immediately after the show. When the singer had concluded his act and taken his bow, he dashed through the pass door into the auditorium, dragged a bewildered Jack Spot from his seat, and the two men became lost in the mêlée of 2,300 people filing out of the theatre.

As Daniels and Spot climbed into the waiting taxi at the front, the six visitors reappeared at the back. 'I'm sorry,' said Cooper, 'but you're just too late. Billy Daniels left by the front entrance to avoid the fans.'

Scarface was not easily convinced. 'Listen, Pop', he growled. 'The show finished two minutes ago. Do as you're told and fetch Jack Como, or we go in.'

Cooper invited the men to inspect the room for themselves. When they discovered their bird had flown, there was some ugly language, but they left without further trouble.

A couple of days later, Jack Spot's photograph stared out from the front pages of the newspapers. 'Jack Spot, the Soho bookmaker, was attacked by masked men outside his flat in Hyde Park Mansions off the Edgware Road this morning,' one report read. 'The men swooped on him as he returned home with his dark-haired wife Rita. It is understood he has razor cuts on his face.' This was something of an understatement. Seventy-eight stitches were sewn into Jack Spot's face and neck. The Palladium drama of a few nights before? Well, it could have been mere coincidence. . . .

Rock 'n' roll singer Jerry Lee Lewis was in for a shock when he appeared at the Palladium in 1972. He had just begun to sing his rock classic 'Whole Lotta Shakin' Going On' when a mystery man with long hair leapt on stage and started singing along with him. Jerry handed him the microphone and stood back in disbelief as the stranger held the audience spellbound for almost five minutes. Dressed in a cord jacket and velvet jeans, the intruder did a quick jig across the stage before finally being escorted back to his seat. The audience applauded and cheered.

As the unknown singer went off, he told the stage manager, 'I'm going to be a star. I'll be playing here one day.' Murray Kash, who was compère for the show said, 'I've never seen anything like it. This boy was good enough to be a professional. And Jerry was so cool that everyone thought the man was part of the act.'

Next day the scene-stealer identified himself as an ex-road sweeper from St. Albans in Hertfordshire. He admitted that this was not the first occasion he had gatecrashed a performance. 'But this is the biggest chance I've ever had. And it was at the Palladium. You can't get much better than that.' Show business magnate Marvyn Conn was impressed. 'The boy's got guts,' he said. 'I'm going to give him an audition, and maybe sign him up for my recording company.'

Peter Noone showed a remarkable display of confidence — or lack of embarrassment — when he appeared at the Palladium with his group, Herman's Hermits. Through almost the whole of his act, his flies were undone.

As for singer Rosemary Clooney, she can claim to have brought the house down — literally. The audience were just settling into their seats when a section of the roof fell in. Two large chunks of plaster dropped into the rear stalls injuring five people. The ceiling was shored up, three hundred seats were roped off, and the show, which included the song 'Ain't Gonna Need This House No Longer', started twenty minutes late. Of the two people who needed hospital treatment after the accident, one headed straight back to the Palladium afterwards to demand his money back.

That night was not the first time the Palladium roof had caved in. During the run of 'The Little Dog Laughed', an electrician working between performances on the roof noticed a crack. When he touched the ceiling it was soggy. George Black cleared his staff from the theatre and the safety curtain was lowered. Hardly was it down when tons of masonry and rubble came crashing to the ground. Twenty-six seats were smashed into pieces. Had it happened during an actual performance, there is little doubt some of the patrons sitting in those seats would have been killed.

A crash of another kind happened while Jimmy 'Schnozzle' Durante was on stage. One of his gags was to sit his drummer in front of a huge mirror. When the drummer played too loudly, Durante would pick up his stool and hurl it at the man. Just as it seemed the stool would smash the mirror, the drummer would stick out his arm and deftly catch it. Except for one night when Durante's aim was somewhat wild — and crash went the mirror.

A punch, and not a stool, was thrown during a visit by Mario Lanza. The temperamental tenor was assigned a personal escort to attend to his every whim. For four days the phlegmatic 'bodyguard' kept Lanza well clear of trouble. On his last night of duty, Lanza turned on him and bellowed, 'What are you doing here?'

'Why, nothing,' came the reply.

'Then what the hell are we paying you for? Take that!' And with that Lanza landed a beautiful right hook. The escort arrived at the Palladium that night sporting a black eye.

The case of the disappearing actor brought a real-life mystery to a Palladium fairy story. Only hours before he was due on stage in the costliest show ever produced at the theatre, the £250,000 hit musical 'Hans Andersen', comedy star Bob Todd vanished. Two letters he posted after leaving his Tunbridge Wells home for the theatre, gave cause for anxiety. One letter was to his wife Monica, the other to the *Daily Mirror*. Both began with the words, 'You will by now know what I have done.' The actor's agent Hugh Alexander said, 'I know it sounds like suicide, but I don't believe that is the case.'

An understudy took over Todd's role in the show as a schoolteacher, and four days passed before the disappearance was reported in the Press. The star of 'Hans Andersen', Tommy Steele, made an impassioned plea to the lost actor from his Palladium dressing-room through the media: 'If Bob wants someone to talk to, I'll meet him at six o'clock tomorrow at the jellied eel stall. He'll know where I mean because we take it in turns to get eels and whelks for each other every night. They're our staple diet. No one else knows which stall we use, so we'll be by ourselves.'

Todd's face was instantly recognisable through his TV appearances with comedians like Benny Hill, Des O'Connor and Dick Emery. Not surprisingly, he was spotted — by some taxi drivers at Holyhead Station in Anglesey. He was wearing a corduroy coat, and carried no luggage. He told the taxi drivers he was on his way to Ireland to make a TV commercial and joked about an understudy taking over his part at the Palladium. One of the drivers took Todd to his home and gave him a Scotch and a cup of tea. 'What am I doing here?' Todd asked. Reminded of what he related earlier, the actor said, 'That's silly. I must be tired.'

Unaware of the dramatic search going on in England, the driver took Todd back to the station where the actor joined the mail boat to Dun Laoghaire. He was not seen again until he walked, unrecognised, into St. Brendan's Psychiatric Hospital in Dublin. The Irish Police circulated his description back to England, and Todd's wife and son flew to Dublin. Doctors diagnosed that his condition was probably due to a slight fracture of the skull, which Todd reckoned must have happened a few weeks earlier when he had fallen on stage. Said his son, Paddy: 'He must still be suffering from the combined effects of the fractured skull and the pressure of doing the Palladium show six nights a week. All he seems worried about now is having his white bed socks that he uses for his Palladium act.'

A few weeks later, well-rested, Todd was back in the show.

The disappearance of Bob Todd was a prominent newspaper story for several days. But another drama surrounding the record-breaking 'Hans Andersen' eluded the newshounds. It happened just forty-eight hours before the opening night, when Tommy Steele blew his top — and the musical director walked out on the show.

The flare-up came late on Saturday evening during the rehearsal of a scene in which a stagecoach taking Hans (Tommy Steele), his ghostly benefactor (Milo O'Shea) and a young midshipman to Copenhagen, was supposed to be transformed into a mighty sailing ship. However, despite three hours' practice the previous night, the changeover was not going well, and Steele rounded furiously on the stagehands. He was unhappy with the music, too, and clashed with the musical director, Alyn Ainsworth. The exchange became heated and Ainsworth walked out.

It could not have happened at a worse moment. The following day had been set aside to cut a long-playing record of the show. The cost of hiring the studio, engaging extra musicians, paying the cast and producing the disc, was a staggering £10,000.

'I'm cancelling the recording,' said Steele, feeling that the company could more usefully spend the time getting the show right.

Long into the night Steele was locked in conversation over the telephone with Harold Fielding, the impresario. Steele argued that there were sixteen imperfections needing to be ironed out before the curtain went up on Monday night; Fielding pledged that the technicians and stage crew would spend the Sunday putting those imperfections right. Meanwhile, the record producer Norman Newell made his own contingency plans, and asked Steele's understudy Barry Hopkins to attend the recording session. Now it was Hopkins's turn to protest. Earlier in the week he had been assured he would not be required for the record, and had made other arrangements.

At home Alyn Ainsworth sat down at his piano. On the music stand stood an unfinished arrangement for one of the show's numbers, 'Jenny Kissed Me'. Any bitterness at the events of the evening was forgotten as he completed the work. Next morning the arrangement was on the musicians' stands at the recording studio. But Ainsworth — who was to have conducted the orchestra — stayed at home.

The traumas of the previous evening were forgotten in the recording studio. Steele turned up, and the session went without a hitch. The most difficult number in the show, 'The King's New Clothes', was recorded in one take.

Meanwhile Harold Fielding was true to his word. Throughout the day he relayed messages to his star that yet another of the sixteen technical faults had been sorted out.

'Hans Andersen' opened on Steele's thirty-eighth birthday — and for the first time, a British audience gave him a standing ovation. The musical ran for ten months, taking more in box office receipts than any Palladium show before it, and then went on a record-breaking tour.

Judy Garland's appearances at the Palladium were as turbulent as her life. Nights of happiness and triumph contrasted with moments of despondency and despair.

In 1950, she lay in hospital, suffering from a nervous breakdown and the constant attempts to keep herself slim. Amongst the telegrams wishing her well was one from Val Parnell. 'We love you as much as ever,' he wrote. 'Come and appear for me as soon as you are well.' Her career was in ruins. She had not worked for five months. Parnell's cable gave her just the fillip she needed to recover. On 9 April 1951, Judy Garland took up Parnell's offer and made her British stage début at the London Palladium.

It was a fraught evening. Judy was nervous and hesitant. Even the audience was tense, willing her to make a triumphant comeback, but fearful lest this should not be the night. As she came to the end of a song, Judy stepped backwards, trod on the hem of her dress, and collapsed in a heap on the stage. The audience sat in shocked silence. Then Judy laughed — and the audience laughed, too. The tension was broken. She sang, 'Over the Rainbow' — and even the hardened stage-hands had tears in their eyes.

Six years later Judy was back at the Palladium for a royal show, which almost ended in a fight with Mario Lanza. Garland was standing with other members of the cast in the wings, anxious to catch a glimpse of the Royal Family's arrival in the box. Lanza joined the group, and stood right in front of her, blocking her view. She politely asked him if he would move to one side, but he refused. Judy was furious. With a few choice expletives, she told Lanza exactly what she thought of him. Not one to shy away from an argument, the Italian singer gave as good as he got. The situation was explosive: the curtain was due to go up at any second. The show's producer stepped between the two combatants, and reminded them that this was not the suitably dignified manner in which to behave on a royal occasion, and peace was restored.

While in Britain in 1963, promoting her new film *I Could Go On Singing,* Judy was invited to top the bill on 'Sunday Night at the London Palladium'. She agreed. But when rehearsals started on Sunday morning, the star was nowhere to be found. Telephone calls were made to her hotel. Assurances were given that Miss Garland would be at the theatre on time, but when the final dress rehearsal was only minutes away, Judy was still missing. Parnell waited quietly in his seat, but the entire company was on a knife's edge, anticipating the clash that must surely come.

Eventually Judy breezed into the theatre as if nothing was amiss. By her side was Dirk Bogarde, the leading man from her film. They were laughing and fooling around. The tension eased, but not for long: when Miss Garland came to rehearse her spot, her mood had changed. She argued with her musical director, then, in the middle of her third number, she rounded on the photographers gathered in front of the stage. 'Get those cameras out of here,' she bellowed. 'I can't concentrate with all that noise going on.' When she finished the song she apologised. 'Sorry, boys. It's okay now.' Bogarde leapt on the stage and hugged Judy. 'That was wonderful,' he said.

She spent the two hours between the final rehearsal and the live performance closeted in her room. The only sound was from a record player — every record a Judy Garland one.

During the show she again stopped the music during the third number. 'The tempo isn't right,' she complained. 'Let's start that again. You see, even at the London Palladium I can stop a song and start again.'

Judy did not make the revolving stage that night. Not, like the Rolling Stones, from deliberate choice — she was drained, emotionally and physically, and her manager stopped her taking that final bow.

On another Palladium occasion, Judy almost didn't make the stage at all. It took an emotional plea from Jimmy Tarbuck to persuade her to appear. 'Listen, darlin',' said Tarbuck. 'They're playing your music. A whole lot of people are going to be terribly disappointed if they don't see you. Just come to the side of the stage with me and see how you feel. Then, if you don't want to go on, forget it. I'll go out and tell them you're not feeling too good, and crack a few gags instead.'

Alfred Marks was the compère for another of her appearances at the Palladium. He counted it a great honour: 'To me she was a super superstar,' he remembers. 'All day long Judy stayed in her dressing-room. I was told she wasn't feeling too well. Just before I was due to make the introduction, I saw her. I got the shock of my life. She looked so ill. I was so overcome, I was on the point of being physically sick. The introduction I fluffed completely. At the side of the stage a large glass of gin was thrust into Judy's hand. She drank it, and someone pushed her on. She was dressed as a tramp, and the audience rose to her. She dangled her legs over the edge

159

of the stage, sang "Walk Down the Avenue" and absolutely captivated that Palladium audience.'

Whenever Judy appeared at the Palladium, one admirer almost took up residence at the stage door. He was in show business himself — a struggling comedian working the provincial halls. He spent most of his spare cash on seats for Judy's shows, and afterwards he always went backstage to see her. 'He was a polite young man,' recalls stage doorkeeper George Cooper. 'I encouraged him to keep working hard. "One day you'll be a star yourself," I told him.'

Many years later, the comedian shot to fame after compèring a Saturday television series. With his new-found wealth he bought a house which he called 'The Garlands' in honour of Judy. In 1974 he was back at the Palladium, no longer the starry-eyed fan, but appearing in his own show and occupying the very dressing-room his idol had used so many times before. Now the Palladium Oscar on the dressing-room door bore a new name: that of Larry Grayson. As the song says, sometimes the dreams that you dare to dream really do come true.

Judy Garland left a legacy of show business talent in her daughters Liza Minnelli and Lorna Luft. Both were to follow their mother onto the Palladium boards — the only theatre in the world where all three Garlands have performed.

Liza shared the spotlight with Judy in 1964, and in 1976 it was Lorna's turn. 'Welcome to the Yellow Brick Road, part three,' she announced to her audience, and sang the Garland classic 'You Made Me Love You', especially for 'Momma'.

The twenty-three year old blonde was honest enough to admit that her Palladium engagement owed much to her mother. 'I'd be fooling myself if I said the audiences are coming to see Lorna Luft,' she said. 'They're coming to see Judy Garland's daughter and Liza Minnelli's sister. But they'll walk away, I hope, liking me. I knew there was a Palladium almost as soon as I knew how to talk. My mother used to tell me wonderful stories about the place. She used to say, "When you've played the Palace on Broadway and the London Palladium, you've done it all." For me, the Palladium was the most terrifying experience of my life, I had to literally grip the curtains for support before going on.'

Lorna's one disappointment when she was asked to play the Palladium was that she would not be given the star dressing-room used by her mother. That had been reserved for Eddie Fisher, who was topping the bill. Throughout the band calls no mention was made of dressing-rooms. After the final rehearsal Lorna went backstage and headed towards the number two room. 'Oh, Miss Luft,' came a shout, 'you've got the star dressing-room.'

With tears in her eyes she walked up to Eddie Fisher and said one word: 'Thanks.' 'There was no need to say what for,' says Lorna.

Each day fan mail poured into that dressing-room, much of it from devotees of Judy Garland, writing of the nights they had sat in the stalls thrilling to the legendary star. One letter was different. It was addressed simply, 'Liza Minnelli, care of Lorna Luft, The London Palladium.'

That's show business.

The Queen

The time is 11 pm. It is a cold, damp November night twenty-four hours before the curtain goes up on Variety's night of the year – the Royal Variety Performance at the London Palladium.

Tomorrow the stalls will be filled with elegant men in dinner jackets and dress suits; elaborately-coiffed ladies in flowing gowns, jewels and furs; the air will be heavy with the scent of expensive perfumes and cigar smoke.

Tonight the audience is less glamorous. The atmosphere is stale, the air reeks of smoke. Workmen with paint pots and brushes are putting the finishing touches to the sprucing-up that always precedes the big night; others in overalls polish away at the brass; steely-eyed security guards check passes and patrol the auditorium; technicians in shirtsleeves are busily fixing microphones, plugging in cables, positioning television cameras. In the stalls, agents and managers and artists and Press men exchange stories *sotto voce*.

On stage, Roy Castle is blowing into a trumpet. Rehearsals, which began with a band call two long days before, are running late. The top of the bill still has to run through his numbers. Tempers are beginning to fray...and Roy Castle's act is not going well. Sir Bernard Delfont, who has presented every Royal Variety Show since 1958, leaps from his seat and steps towards the front of the stage. 'Unless this man puts his act together, he's out,' Delfont storms.

Suddenly the atmosphere becomes electric. Roy Castle, Delfont, the show's producer, Robert Nesbitt, and the artist's agent, Cyril Berlin, go into a huddle on the apron of the stage. Changes are discussed. Roy insists he can come up with another routine by morning. 'All I have to do is collect my band parts,' he says. After ten minutes the group breaks up. Roy Castle walks off dejectedly. The experience would be shattering before any show: before a Royal Show it is a disaster.

Roy Castle had made three cabaret appearances that week, and spent almost the whole of that day in a television studio. 'My mind was still on the TV show,' he says. 'When I got to the Palladium I was expecting a band call, not a full rehearsal. The act was planned in my mind, but there just hadn't been time to put it together. I knew I could go out there and do my stage act, and that it would go down well. But I desperately wanted to give the audience something new. The Royal Variety Performance is a shop window. It's just about the last place on earth you want to do a bad show.' His knees were 'like jelly' as he headed for home that Sunday night. 'I didn't sleep the whole night. I was physically sick. I really didn't want to go on. I wanted to shout: "Please, will someone stand in for me?" '

That night was a sleepless one for three other men, too. In a small reception room behind the Royal Box, Cyril Berlin, Palladium boss Louis Benjamin and leading agent Billy Marsh, discussed together how Castle's act could be reshaped in time for the show. When they emerged in the early hours of the morning, they had a formula to present to the artist. 'Roy is such a good pro that he appreciated we were genuinely trying to help,' says Benjamin.

It was all so different from Roy Castle's first Royal Show in 1958, when he was the young unknown from Huddersfield who had stolen the headlines and beamed out from every front page: 'The show name of the year,' said the newspapers. 'It was all so tame, then new boy Roy perked up the show.' It must have been some performance, considering his fellow artists included Eartha Kitt, Julie Andrews, Rex Harrison, Pat Boone, Norman Wisdom, Bruce Forsyth, Max Bygraves, Tony Hancock and Frankie Vaughan. Castle had been plucked straight out of his first London show at the Prince of Wales theatre to appear in the Royal Variety Performance. Now, sixteen years later, it was an apprehensive Roy Castle who ran through his revamped act on Monday morning. The consensus of opinion was that it was much better. Now came the agonising wait in the theatre until the actual performance that evening in front of the Queen Mother and Lord Snowdon. Castle spent most of the day in his stage costume, pacing the corridors backstage. In the dressing-room he shared with the other comics on the bill, Ted Rogers was running through his topical gags, George Carl was practising his hat-juggling routine, and Billy Dainty was just clowning.

There was one more test of nerves. The running order of the show was changed. Roy found himself switched with George Carl on the bill.

The show had been going well. Rogers, Dainty and impressionist Paul Melba had all won generous applause. Castle stood in the wings, perspiration on his forehead, tight knots of tension in his stomach. 'You can never say you are an old warhorse,' he says. 'For me it gets worse every time.'

Ted Rogers did the introduction, 'My old mate, and one of the nicest guys in show business — Roy Castle.' And Castle walked on, played the Trumpet Voluntary with one finger, told a couple of stories and went into a complex comedy drum routine with his three musicians. He went off to a tremendous ovation — shades of 1958, when Harry Secombe had to push him back on stage to take a second bow.

In the star dressing-room later, Sir Bernard Delfont and Perry Como reflected on the performance. Which act did Como enjoy most? 'George Carl was marvellous,' he said. 'And that British boy who played the drums. He was wonderful. So much talent.'

Delfont puffed at his huge cigar. 'We had a bit of trouble with that act,' he mused. 'That boy has so much talent, but he can't harness it. I made him do this, that and the other, and it worked. The Queen Mother said this is the best Royal Show she's seen for many years — and we made a record £50,000.'

'Oh yes?' replied Como, deadpan. 'And who is going to pay me?'

In the comics' room — Number G at the end of the corridor — it was all smiles, congratulations and light-hearted banter. The five occupants had done well, and they knew it. Roy Castle could be forgiven if his smile was the broadest. 'I knew deep down that it would turn out all right.' he confessed. 'This is my lucky room. I was here for a show with Morecambe and Wise, and one evening Eric and his wife invited me out on a foursome. I said I would love to go, but I had nobody to invite. Eric went off, made a telephone call to the Palace Theatre, and returned to say he had fixed a blind date. A friend of the Morecambes called Fiona, who was appearing in 'The Sound of Music', had agreed to make up the foursome.' As it turned out, it was his first date with the girl who was to become his wife.

Several days after the Royal Show, Roy Castle sent a telegram to Louis Benjamin. It recalled an occasion when Roy was a struggling comedian and Benjamin the general manager of the Winter Gardens in Morecambe. Benjamin had been allocated only £50 — excluding the star's salary — to put together an entire Variety bill. Roy Castle begged him to put him in the show. Benjamin explained that he had run out of money, but seeing the disappointment on the young comic's face he agreed to book him for four spots for £2 — just ten shillings a spot. Castle jumped at the offer. His cryptic telegram after the Royal Show said simply, 'Do you think I'm worth double figures now?'

As Roy Castle's experience illustrates, there is no show more nerve-wracking for an entertainer than the Royal Variety Performance.

'It affects artists in different ways,' says Ken Dodd. 'Some become talkative; some go quiet and morose. Personally, my top lip sticks to my teeth.'

Harry Secombe, veteran of eight Royal Variety Shows, says, 'Some of the most relaxed and composed-looking people are a bundle of nerves. I have seen Bob Hope pacing up and down like a caged tiger. I think we do it as a kind of masochistic pleasure. If you are an established star all you can hope for is to get away with it. You never enhance your reputation. It's a night of anticipation and hope for the youngster. A night of nerve-wracking anxiety for the established performer. I try to break the tension by blowing a raspberry.'

As Tommy Cooper walked off after his act one year, a quaking fellow artist asked him, 'What's it like out there, Tommy?' 'Packed,' came the reply.

Tony Hancock was physically sick, and Gilbert Harding needed so much Dutch courage before playing a butler in a Royal Show sketch, that he had to be strapped to a cocktail trolley and pushed on.

Will Mahoney, an American who danced on a xylophone, was a sensation when he appeared in Variety at the Palladium, taking an unprecedented seventeen curtain calls. Yet when the National Anthem was played at the start of the 1935 Royal Show he became so paralysed with fear that he spent the two hours before his entrance flat on his xylophone at the back of the stage.

Producers of Royal Shows have to be ever mindful that nothing in an artist's performance should give offence. In 1912 Queen Mary turned her face from the stage, shocked by the sight of Vesta Tilley in trousers performing as a male impersonator. In the 'twenties, chorus girls were not permitted to appear without wearing stockings. A far cry from the Royal Show of 1975, when a group of Zulu dancers appeared bare-breasted. After all, as Buckingham Palace told the Kwa Zulu group, 'The Queen has seen plenty of topless dancers on her world tours.'

Paradoxically, in the same show, French singing star Charles Aznavour was ordered to drop a controversial number he had sung in rehearsals. Called 'What Is Man', the song described the sad life led by a homosexual. 'I was politely asked if I could find another song,' says Aznavour. 'It was a nice way of informing me that the Queen might be offended.'

Today, though, it is mostly the comedians who suffer the blue pencil treatment. For them, censorship has become stricter. The Crazy Gang could get away with outrageous conduct and material during their long reign as Royal Show favourites. In 1950 Tommy Trinder and the Gang were sent out before the show to warm up the audience, always regarded as particularly stiff and difficult to break down. Trinder came on first, and pulled a sheaf of press clippings from his pocket. 'I'm going to read your notices from last year,' he told the audience. 'If I'd had such lousy write-ups I'd never show my face inside a theatre again.' The Crazy Gang then marched on with mallets, cricket bats and golf clubs and threatened to hit anyone who did not laugh. Bud Flanagan and Teddy Knox, dressed as charwomen, went into the Royal Box and began tidying up. Flanagan threw a programme onto the stage. Trinder picked it up, feigned amazement, and said, 'Shows how often they clean this theatre. This a programme for Hengler's Circus.'

The tables were turned on Flanagan and Allen during a Royal Show rehearsal. As they walked on stage to the familiar strains of 'Underneath the Arches', a loud raspberry came from the direction of the Royal Box. Flanagan and Allen and everyone else in the theatre, stared up in disbelief. Seated in the box were Jimmy Nervo in a blonde wig and with a coloured rug draped around his shoulders, and Charlie Naughton in a cloak trimmed with ermine and a crown that flopped jauntily over one eye. Even the Lord Chamberlain — at the rehearsal to censor any dubious material — joined in the laughter.

It was the Queen Mother who saved Tommy Steele's bacon during his first Royal Show appearance. When Steele invited the audience to clap their hands along with his hit song, 'Singing the Blues', they sat motionless in their seats. 'I was dying on my feet,' he recalls. 'Then, bless 'er, the Queen Mum realised what was 'appening, leaned over the

Royal Box, and started to clap 'er 'ands. Within seconds the audience — who traditionally take their cue from the Royal Box — were clapping along too.'

Ted Rogers prepared a number of royal gags for the 1974 performance, but Sir Bernard Delfont censored them. It was around the time that newspapers were speculating on a new romance between Richard Burton and a princess who was the estranged wife of a Tory parliamentary candidate. 'If Richard Burton marries Princess Elizabeth of Yugoslavia, he could be sitting up there in the Royal Box next year,' joked Rogers. 'Out!' said Delfont. Another gag poked gentle fun at the other artists on the bill: 'What with Perry Como (aged 62), and Josephine Baker (68), appearing, they were thinking of re-naming it "Senior Showtime".' 'Out!' said Delfont.

The Delfont axe also fell on Paul Melba, one of the stars of television's 'Who Do You Do?'. Melba was told to drop his impersonation of Prince Philip, one of the high spots of his cabaret act, and although he squeezed in an impression of the show's star, Perry Como, at rehearsal, it was cut from the actual performance.

Backstage, Sir Bernard explained the reasons for his censorship, 'I just felt the whole thing had gone too far,' he said. 'Comics were vying with each other to tell the most outrageous joke, trying to score off the Royal Family. The days of the Crazy Gang are past. They could get away with it, but there are few comedians who can do that today'.

Norman Vaughan was one of the few. It was during the days when motorists cluttered their rear windows with holiday stickers. 'There's a smashing car outside,' said Norman. 'Don't know who it belongs to, but the stickers on the back say Windsor, Balmoral and Sandringham.' He was less successful with another gag. This time it was not the words, but a gesture that was objected to. 'I was following a magician who did several vanishing tricks with a large white handker-chief,' said Vaughan. 'I planned to walk on, carefully take a handkerchief from my pocket, show each side to the audience, magician-style, raise it slowly to my face — and blow my nose.' But he was told to cut it, and when he asked why, was told: 'We can't have an artist blowing his nose in front of the Queen.'

Royal Variety Shows are often referred to as Command Performances. This title is a misnomer: there have been only two Commands. The first was on 1 July 1912 at the Palace Theatre in London's Shaftesbury Avenue. King George V asked the music hall profession to stage a gala occasion which he and his wife would attend. The profession was delighted. Royal recognition meant the 'illegitimate' child of the arts had become 'legit'. They responded by lining up the greatest galaxy of stars ever to appear at one performance. Of the music hall artists of the day, only Marie Lloyd (still considered too coarse for the royal palate) and Albert Chevalier (who took out a full-page newspaper advertisement to register his protest) were missing from the grand finale, in which 142 performers were assembled on stage.

Harry Lauder sang 'Roamin' in the Gloamin' '; George Robey came on as the Mayor of Mudcumdyke, the curtain dropped prematurely and unceremoniously on Charles Aldrich in the middle of his impersonations, and Harry Claff donned the armour and sword of the White Knight to give a solo of 'God Save the King'.

The second Command Performance was at the London Coliseum on 28 July 1919 in celebration of peace, and in appreciation of the generous manner in which Variety artists had assisted the 1914-18 war fund. His Majesty expressed a wish that the proceeds should go to a charity of the Variety profession. Sir Oswald Stoll selected the Variety Artistes' Benevolent Fund. The evening was so successful that the profession decided to make it an annual event and royal patronage was granted. The Variety Artistes' Benevolent Fund has been the beneficiary of every subsequent Royal Show — the proceeds going almost entirely to finance the Fund's home for retired entertainers at Brinsworth House in Twickenham. The fund has since been renamed the Entertainment Artistes' Benevolent Fund.

The first Royal Variety Performance, as we now know it, was held on 25 November 1921. The public was apathetic. The sale of tickets, priced up to three guineas — in 1975 the price of the most expensive seats was increased from £40 to £50 — was slow until the engagement was announced of the Princess Royal and the Earl of Harewood. The couple decided their first public appearance together would be at the Royal Variety Show, and the happy event guaranteed a full house.

The Hippodrome, Coliseum, Victoria Palace and Alhambra theatres were the venues for the show until 1930, when George Black offered the use of his Palladium.

When King George V and Queen Mary sat in the Royal Box in 1930 they were entertained by such music hall greats as Tom Payne and Vera Hilliard, George Clarke, Julian Rose, De Groot, Gillie Potter ('speaking to you in English from Hogsnorton'), Max Wall (who, in 1974, made a sensational comeback at the Palladium and went on to star in his own one-man West End show), Nervo and Knox, Will Hay, Jack Payne and his Band, and Coram the ventriloquist (who always dressed as an army officer and had a soldier dummy called Jerry).

To be chosen for a Royal Variety Performance is the highest accolade an artist can be given. Contracted engagements permitting, it is rare for a performer to decline an invitation to appear, and international stars fly to London from all over the world especially for this one show.

Duke Ellington gave one of his last performances with his band in the 1973 Royal Show (he died a few months later). They arrived at their hotel with hand luggage only, having arranged for their heavy baggage to be dispatched separately. When the curtain went up on Royal Show night, the luggage had still not arrived; this posed quite a problem, for the trunks contained not only the band's stage outfits, but also their music and their instruments. The band had already been forced to skip rehearsals and it looked as if they might have to miss the performance, too. Frantic phone calls were made. The Royal Show was well into its first half when a van pulled up outside the Palladium with the priceless trunks.

The Royal Family has no direct say in the choice of artists, although the members sometimes let it be known that there is a particular act they would like to see. The composition of the show is the prerogative of Sir Bernard Delfont, president of the Entertainment Artistes' Benevolent Fund. But if royalty has been reticent about the choice of artists, one monarch made his feelings known about the timing of the show in no uncertain manner. King George VI sent for George Black to inquire what time the curtain would come down. The show was running late, but Black confidently predicted, 'Oh, I should say about 11 pm, sir.' 'That's ten minutes too long', replied the King. 'This show must be over by 10.30 pm. There are scores of police lining the route to Buckingham Palace and I don't want them kept waiting a moment longer than is necessary. Anyway, the staff at the Palace have been told that we shall be home by eleven.'

Unlike her late husband, the Queen Mother was in no such hurry during the 1974 performance. During the intermission she inquired whether the audience had returned to their seats for the second half, as the curtain was due to go up. 'No', Sir Bernard Delfont informed her. 'We can't get them out of bars'. 'Oh, well,' said the Queen Mother, 'let them enjoy themselves for a little longer then.'

The most traumatic night in the Royal Show's history was 5 November 1956, the weekend of the Suez crisis. Val Parnell told the assembled company that, because of the landings in the Middle East, the Queen had been advised not to attend the performance. Parnell left it to the artists to decide whether the show should go ahead. They talked it over and decided that without the Queen's presence the show would not be a Royal Performance in the true sense of the words.

Harry Secombe was appearing every night at the Palladium in 'Rocking the Town', and had acquired a goodly supply of liquor for the artists who were to share his dressing-room on the royal night. Soon quite a crowd had gathered to drown their sorrows in his room, and a party was in full swing. A message was delivered that Liberace was in his dressing-room in tears. He had come to Britain especially for the royal occasion, and when Secombe's crowd reached Liberace's room they found him weeping openly and unashamedly. He was persuaded to join the party, but nothing could raise his spirits. Jimmy Wheeler was becoming maudlin. 'I'm going to do my act if it kills me,' he said, and picking up his violin he ran through his entire Royal Show script. By the end of it, Liberace was hysterical with laughter.

As a finale to every Royal Show, the artists line up in the foyer to be introduced to the distinguished guests. Many artists prefer their after-show conversations with royalty to remain private; others are genuinely too nervous to remember what was said. One poor fellow actually curtsied instead of bowing.

Des O'Connor was struck dumb when he met the Queen Mother. 'You seem to be enjoying yourself, Mr O'Connor,' she said. As hard as he tried, the comedian could not utter one intelligible word.

Royal visitors are usually well briefed on where the artists are appearing, but when the Queen Mother was introduced to Peter Sellers she was unsure.

'What are you doing at the moment, Mr. Sellers?' she asked.

'Standing here, ma'am,' he told her in all seriousness.

Impressionist Mike Yarwood has never quite decided what the Queen Mother meant when she told him after one show, 'It really is quite frightening how you appear to become Harold Wilson.'

The classic royal exchange must belong to Tommy Trinder when he met King George VI. Trinder reminded the King that the last occasion he had entertained him was eight years before, when the King was still the Duke of York.

'You've done pretty well since those days,' said the King, noting that Trinder was topping the bill at the Palladium.

'And you haven't done so badly yourself, sir,' said Trinder.

The show is over. The curtain has come down. Slowly the audience wends its way to the waiting cars, taxis, buses and tubes. There really is nothing more to be said, except that I hope your visit in print to the London Palladium has been an enjoyable one.

In ten minutes time the curtain will rise again on the second house. Should you wish to stay, there is no extra charge. Just flick back the pages and start reading all over again.

Acknowledgements

I am grateful to the following artists who have kindly co-operated in the writing of this book:

Barbara Aitken
Arthur Askey
George Carl
Roy Castle
Billy Dainty
Ken Dodd
Gracie Fields
Colette Gleeson
Peter Goodwright
Noele Gordon
Barry Hopkins
Jimmy Jewel
Lorna Luft
Alfred Marks

Eric Morecambe
Debbie Reynolds
Ted Rogers
Harry Secombe
Dorothy Squires
Tommy Steele
Tiller Girls
Bob Todd
Frankie Vaughan
Norman Vaughan
Jack Warner

I would also like to thank:

Louis Benjamin, managing director, Moss Empires.
Jack Benson, head flyman (retired), Palladium.
Ron Harris, property master, Palladium.
Tommy Hayes, stage director, Palladium.
Albert J. Knight
Albert Locke
Robert Luff
Robert Nesbitt
Jim Smith, floor manager, ATV.
Yvonne Stoll, Press Officer, ATV.
Rose Summers, housekeeper, Palladium.
Ron Swift, general manager, Palladium.
Eric Tann, musical supervisor, Moss Empires.
Brenda Thomas, advertising manager, Moss Empires.
And all the Palladium staff.

My special thanks to:

George Cooper, former stage doorkeeper, Palladium, for his many reminiscences.

Ian Bevan, author of an earlier book on the Palladium, *Top of the Bill*, from which the facts for much of the early history have been gleaned.

Tony Wells, press officer for Moss Empires, and his assistant 'Bobby' Robi for their valued help.

Mellanie, Trudi and Simon for their encouragement and patience. And Ethel and Bill Pilton, who first took me to the London Palladium as a kid in short trousers.

175